SELECTED STORIES

Selected Stories

by

Mark Valentine

Swan River Press
Dublin, Ireland
MMXXI

Selected Stories
by Mark Valentine

Published by
Swan River Press
Dublin, Ireland
in April, MMXXI

www.swanriverpress.ie
brian@swanriverpress.ie

Cover design by Meggan Kehrli from
"The Gold Mask" (2012) by Jason Zerrillo.

Set in Garamond by Ken Mackenzie

Paperback Edition
ISBN 978-1-78380-742-0

Swan River Press published a limited hardback
edition of *Selected Stories* in November 2012.

Contents

To
Guy Sydney Niall Valentine
of Co. Cork

A Certain Power

I. The Collector

In a remote corner of the city, on a dark narrow inlet of the great river, there huddled a row of oddly-shaped cottages called the Dutch houses, the last relic of mad Peter's Netherlandish infatuation. They were made of a brick once old rose in colour, but over the decades the rose had become blighted by scars of black and streaks of green, from grime and decay. Their roof-lines were curved like a serpent's back. They each possessed, set in the middle of the arching gables, a round oriel window of nine small panes, but not one of the four houses had glass in every pane; sacking or a hacking of wood patched the gaps. For, notwithstanding their history, this ancient quartet (ancient by the standards of the eighteenth century "new city", as they were amongst the first to be built there), were never home to anyone prosperous or eminent; the miasma from the sullenly lapping waters of this trapped reach of the river was enough to ensure that.

And, too, it was as if here the command of the city's founder against the domain of the marshes had not quite been obeyed to the full; here, they stole back at its uttermost edges, silently and slowly, patiently, and turned the tracks queachy, the air treacherous, and the mists, the many mists, into a greenish-yellow, sulphurous presence, a livid, living, hovering slime. So, in this fetid, shunned, forgotten backwater, the Revolution did not reach; and nor, when it came, did the liberation by the forces of the Free Baltic. Whether it was a Tsar, a Commissar or an International Commissioner who ruled the city was a matter of no moment here, or not very much. Food was hard to get, or it could be got; alcohol and oil could be obtained from the shelves of the shack of a shop nearby, or it could be secured only in darkness at the least-known wharves, from strangers. Those were the changes that were noticed by the inhabitants of the Dutch houses.

One evening, at dusk, in among the hanging ichors of malachite and ochre that pervaded the inlet, a different hue could be discerned, as if a new element had coalesced from their reactions; a dark arrow. It drove through the clammy veils with a purpose and a force, like a shadow set free, no longer a dim echo of light, but allowed, under some inscrutable dispensation, to have its own way. And shortly after, the bronze bell of the fourth and last of the Dutch houses clanged: and Mr. Kournos, grumbling to himself, slowly undid the locks and latches and peered out. He saw a young man in dark garb, in an all-enveloping cloak held by a heraldic button he could not quite make out. Were it not for that emblem, he might have taken him for a priest of some kind (and there were many different kinds in the city now, that much Mr. Kournos knew). The stranger wore his hair long and it laced around his shoulders and nape, so that, to the owner of the fourth and last cottage, it looked like the mane of a great black lion. And this image was reinforced by the watchful solemn eyes of his visitor, which were also those of a cat-of-prey. So, all in all, whether this man were a priest or an official, Mr. Kournos thought he ought to let him in, things being as they now were in the city.

Each of the Dutch houses had a room—called simply "the room"—where such few visitors as ever arrived could be adequately received. A Dutch stove with painted tiles reigned here like a voracious fire-idol, and into its maw, when they could afford it, the occupants fed such fuel as they could find. When that was not easy, the cottage-dwellers so far co-operated, despite a natural reticence, as to keep one stove going in one house at a time, by turns, and here they would all congregate, in silence mostly: Mr. Kournos, who was a retired merchant; the boatman, who plied a trade to the outer islands; the scholar; and the old dancer, Madame Helena, who lent the gathering such grace and sophistication as it had, in and among the rough naïvety of the men. After a time, they would share some of their food and drink too, and—with the ballerina's permission—pipes of the Ottoman tobacco that had mysteriously arrived in great cotton bales at the number fourteen wharf some weeks ago.

But on this occasion, Mr. Kournos was alone. The young man that he called to himself "the black lion" declined a glass of tea or even to take a seat on the old draped couch. He was civil, but he was also quite curt.

"Well, Meinheer,"—he paused to see if the little jest at the Dutchness of the house had been appreciated— "well, Meinheer, it is like this. You bought a sack of firewood from a furtive scoundrel of sorts on the outer island, and only a few nights ago. Now, if you have not burnt it, I want that sack and I will pay well for it, in the New Roubles or the Old, whichever you prefer, or indeed in any form that suits you."

Too old, too cautious, even in this rank backwater, to admit to anything or to agree too readily a price for anything, Mr. Kournos stroked his white beard and tried to return the stranger's stare, before looking away.

"Is firewood so hard to come by again then?" he asked. There was a pause.

"This firewood is. It's quite possible, though, that I will not want the whole sack-full. I may just want to look at it and there might, or might not, be a stick or two I should like to take away. I will pay you the same, whatever the case." The stranger's dark, shining stare, in which the gleam of fierceness and the veil of ennui seemed to vie for possession, stayed levelled at him, but even then the "Meinheer" was not to be hurried. If this "black lion" wanted this bag of sticks so keenly, then it must have an unusual value. But what value? What could there be in a crack of wood? The sack was stored in the dim lower recesses of a painted cupboard in a corner of the room, and he did not know himself exactly what was in it, other than that it weighed and rattled like the tinder it was supposed to be. Not by a single flicker of his gaze did Mr. Kournos allow his eyes to betray where the firewood was stored, though. Instead, he regarded the dark young man gravely and decided it was his turn to ask questions.

"You are an investigator from the International Commission, no doubt? You are wasting your time. No agitators, no speculators, no black marketeers, no conspirators live here. Why would they? We are all simple folk, getting by. We exist, simply, in among the mist. Surely that is not a crime in the eyes of the world even now?"

The black, black eyes did not blink. "I am searching, Meinheer, but not on behalf of the Commission. Even though all the nations of the world seem to have gathered in this city to be its safeguard against the red terror, even so I am from, shall we say, another power, a certain power, that has other interests. If I assure you of our protection, will that help?"

Mr. Kournos considered further. Unless this stranger was a lunatic, in which case it might be better to humour him, then who could say which of the many agencies in the city he might represent, and what influence he might wield? They all had their shadowy presence. He might be an American, or an Abyssinian, or an Armenian, or . . .

Sighing, he spread out on the flagged floor with the faded Caspian rug some sheets from the *Chronicle of Current Events*. Then he reached into the cupboard and dragged out the sack. A few deft cuts of his pocket knife and the cords were broken. He heaved the sack upside down and watched its mouth disgorge its contents, with a brittle rattling. And then he drew his breath in sharply.

Upon the stale newspaper pages there had risen a pyre of blazing colour. Scarlet, gold, royal blue, sepia, gleaming white, shining black; and as he stared the colours revealed forms; eyes, wings, beards, tears, birds, flowers, hands, cloaks, gems, wounds, and most of all light, light in silver, gilt, amber, in snow and in blood.

Mr. Kournos stretched out a reluctant hand as if to pick up one of the vivid shards, but drew back, as if they were real flames. But he was not to be spared so easily. The stranger said: "Will you turn them all over for me, carefully? I want to look for something in particular."

"Sir," the old man began, "I had no idea . . . "

But the stranger shook his black mane brusquely. "Of course not. They took them all and shattered them in their retreat. What they could not burn, they broke. Still, these are after all just paint and wood. They did more to flesh and blood."

Very cautiously, using only the utter tips of his fingers, and very gently and slowly, Mr. Kournos laid out the brilliant splinters one by one, like so many brightly dressed puppets in a paper mortuary. The "black lion" regarded them carefully.

At length, all had been displayed, and the occupant of the fourth and last Dutch house allowed himself to advance once more a question.

"You—are looking for one in particular?"

"Yes—for one in particular."

"It is not here?"

"No."

"And how could you know it, from such fragments?"

The dark young man smiled.

"I will be able to tell. Call it the style of the brush stroke, if you like, or certain tints in the colouring, or the grain of the wood, which they say was cypress, and very rare. Or say, rather, simply that I will *know*."

"You are a collector then?" A glimmer of light bloomed in the old man's mind. That sort of business he understood. Why hadn't he said?

But his visitor seemed to find his remark especially amusing, even if the enjoyment did not exactly reach his eyes.

"Yes, I am a collector." And then the old man felt a stare like the stare of a son of Medusa, and was suddenly very weary. A black film descended like a blindfold over his eyes, and he heard the words, slow and solemn and simple, resound in his head: "But not yet of you." And so that is why it was that some moments later the blackness left him, or perhaps only mostly left him, and he found the stranger had left too.

II. *The Enlightener*

Afterwards, they discussed who she was. A spy, some thought; a noblewoman come to join the workers' struggle, said others; a high revolutionary official, said the shrewd, perhaps from the Commissar for Enlightenment? And why? Because she showed such interest in how and where the breaking of the idols and desecration of the shrines had been done. Who else, but one whose job it was to advance education and banish superstition, could be so concerned, especially in these desperate times, when the workers were all but surrounded in their heartland, now that the city had fallen to the forces of world capital, the primitive tribes ruled in the South, and Siberia was the preserve of the imperialists? Yes, she was making sure they had done a thorough job of it, so that there would be one victory at least, so that the priests had nothing but hollow empty shells to carry out their mummery in.

She had come to a certain bar in the outer island, where the sway of the internationals was still at its least, and in that den the axe-boned, unshaven men, dispirited and downbeaten, consoled themselves with the coarse potato-spirit they passed off as vodka. Their hands were grained and calloused, pitted and worn like the rough wooden tables in the bar. For greater discretion, or from parsimony, or both, the lamps of the bar were few and feebly lit, so that a gloom reigned. Men mostly sat alone, staring at their glass or at their hands or at the darkness. Where there was a knot of men together, perhaps in one of the hollowed-out recesses, the voices rarely rose above a murmur, even when in drink. Not even the women of the streets came here very much, except in the most desperation: they had learnt the men had no money to offer and nothing to barter; and, in any case, now that the occupying forces thronged the city, there was no shortage of trade. So, when she came through the door, a restive excitement broiled inside the men, along with a resentment that she should presume to enter their domain, the last secret redoubt of those who had thought they might take an entire empire.

She wore the dark tunic and breeches of the workers, and stout boots streaked with the green spittle of the gutter and caked with the Baltic salt from the waters that lapped the low shores of the island. Her hair was fiercely tied up under a slouching cap. All of her was in black, with only a pinprick gleam of light from some emblem or other above the peak of the cap, which they could not make out in the dimness: when she tilted her head, it glinted like a facet of coal. Yet against the blackness of her clothes, her face and neck and hands were a bright white, even if streaked here and there with grime. She was very slender and spare, and the bones of her face stood starkly through the pale flesh; and if it had not been for this evidence of her hunger and deprivation, it is doubtful the workmen would have confided in her. But it was plain to see that she had suffered too, and not just in the sharp shards of her face, but in her eyes, which were like cinders.

Yes, afterwards, old Harkov, a veteran, thought about how she had appeared before them, and her brittleness and the way the whiteness of her flesh and the blackness of her garb contrasted, and he said to himself, for he came from the country originally, that she was like the birch trees that had grown in their groves of silver and shadow for many versts, so many versts, taut and angular and tall against whatever the winds might do. That is how she was too, he thought. And tales from his childhood came into his head, about how the she-spirits of those trees could be set free to walk among men, but seldom to their advantage; and he shuddered inside his ragged greatcoat and sunk himself deeper into it, and cradled the shot glass in his palms.

Yet, he reflected, he had never heard that such a spirit would be interested in politics. Still, in these times . . . For she had questioned him, as she had questioned the others, gently, confidingly, in kind whispers, about the way they had gone about carrying out the final order before the workers' forces had decided to make a—what did they call it? He had searched carefully for the correct term: a strategic regrouping, something like that. Anyhow, they had left. And that order? Yes, they had done it. So which, precisely, of the god-houses, she wanted to know had been stripped, by which unit or detachment, and what had they done with what they found? Had it all been destroyed?"

Here, it is true, even in response to her soft voice, which seemed to steal into their minds like a spring breeze, some of them became a little restless, their jaws tightened and their eyes narrowed. But something about her persuasion, and her vulnerability, and her earnestness, moved even these to make some grudging admissions. It was obvious there had been things of worth there, and they were very poor; and the movement needed funds too; if only, for instance, there had been more rifles and shells, they might not be sitting here today and they could have thrown the bandits back.

It was possible, they said, that some of the superstitious trappings had been sold. Not, of course, to the priests or nobles, though it must be said these had approached them, through go-betweens. Certainly not to them, those crows and peacocks, no. To—to merchants, traders, dealers. And then they found that they had somehow named those who had paid. After all, could that do harm?

Some of them became a little uneasy and thought they had better make more sure of who she was. So they had asked her, "are you, then, an enlightener?", using the faintly scoffing name they gave to the worker educationalists they sent amongst them. And then her thin pale lips had curved slightly and she had said, yes, you could say she was an enlightener, indeed. That seemed to comfort them, and they gave her a certain admiration for her bravery in still working in the city when it was under the occupation of capital.

Then the door of that bar on the outer island had opened, and the thrusts of cold air that came in were so intense they were like an icy heat: and it was as if the guttering black shadows within were reinforced by a greater blackness. The questioned men, still solemnly wondering what she wanted from them, had huddled and crouched even further back in the face of this blast; and when they looked up, she had gone. Then the room seemed blacker and colder than ever.

III. *The Liberator*

Of course, it was not quite like the former days, probably it never could be quite like those days of dignity, yet it had some of their fine old flavour, and the two Countesses were determined to enjoy it, in the court gowns they had saved from the ravages of what they could only bring themselves to describe as "the madness". If their jewels were more of glass and paste than before, if their satin shoes were still a little scuffed from departures in haste, if their lorgnettes drooped a little forlornly on their hinges, still their backs were straight and their eyes, quartering the room for indications of rank or character, were as keen as ever.

They listened only vaguely to the little speech some functionary of the International Commission was making, trying to pay tribute to each of the forces in turn. "The great Tsar who founded this city more than two hundred years ago looked to Europe for his inspiration, for the standards of civilisation. Now his worthy successors in Russia, aided by the great European nations, and the new nations, have together thrust back the forces of red barbarism. Surely a greater destiny yet awaits us here in our new role as an International City, the first in the world. Who can doubt . . . "

Their attention wandered. A discreet gesture of a coiffured head (for the hairdressers had never deserted them)—

"Over there—the soldier. Such a handsome, cruel face. Like a sparrowhawk, my angel, don't you think?"

"Where? Ah, I see. Indeed. Such a beautiful dark uniform too. So very black. I do not think I have ever seen anything quite so utterly black. Unless . . . " A little moue of the carmine lips. "It reminds me of that lovely velvety black that Tiziano Vecelli so loved to employ in his portraits. Which power do you think he serves?"

"Oh, who knows, dear. So many armies here, we ought to feel quite safe."

"German, do you think?"

"No, my darling; observe, no duelling scar."

"Ah. Then French . . . "

"Mmm. Elegant, but not quite elegant enough, you know. And no pomade."

"Then English?"

"My dear! Do you detect the smell of rain, old dogs and vile pipe tobacco?"

There was a slight quivering of well-bred nostrils.

"No? Then decidedly not."

"Too much of a mystery, then, Countess. Unless—a Finn?"

"Possibly a Finn. They say we owe it all to them. And certainly, my dear, better Finnish than *finis*, you know? And yet . . . do you not think there is something more *fire* than ice there ?"

"He has a little emblem at his collar, but I cannot—" the frail lorgnette was raised to the watery blue eyes, . . . " . . . no, I cannot make it out."

"Then let us perambulate and see what the others have found out about him. Such a face, such a figure, and such *eyes* . . . "

The soldier, meanwhile, had allowed himself to be captured by a soulful young woman in a crepe dress of faded gold, with filigree as brittle and delicate as dried flowers. She seemed to carry a train of devotees, who listened admiringly, and the Countesses stationed themselves at the outer fringes of this coterie.

"You are one of our liberators, sir?" she asked.

A smile of deprecation illumined the soldier's face.

"Yes, I have been called a liberator. I am the envoy of, shall we say, a certain power."

("Aha, a diplomat as well as a soldier, you see," said one Countess. "And his accent quite faultless," returned the other.)

"One would not wish in the least to diminish the role of those gallant soldiers who came to our aid," (here a nod to the officer), said the young woman, "but we must see too that it was fore-ordained. All the signs of Antichrist have come among us and it could not be long before the Sword of Saint Michael was raised in our defence."

The two Countesses nudged one another.

"She evidently hasn't seen the angel's generals then."

"No?"

"Well—an egg and a walnut, with a moustache like a hasty signature on each. Nothing gilded, winged and glorious about them."

All of the acolytes in the train of the young woman nodded, and one, a little man with a pointed beard and a pince-nez perilously perched on a narrow nose, decided to be more zealous still.

"Ah, Princess, how true. And if one of the great host has come to our aid, may we not confidently expect the others? Saint Raphael will bring us his healing, Saint Uriel . . . " (there was a pause) . . . . his own special, um, powers, and Saint Gabriel certainly a message of hope."

The two sceptical beldames had insinuated themselves through the little gathering so that they were decidedly more adjacent to the mysterious soldier. But before turning their attention to him, they could not resist a further commentary.

"I am rather afraid, dear, that Saint Gabriel will be quite out of countenance with us, you know. You remember that exquisite wonder-working picture of him in the little church in the east of the city?"

"I do: a wonderful effect of silk and gold. And such locks, and such a sweet face. If only to have met the model . . . "

"To do that, my cherished one, you would need to have lived four or five hundred years ago, and even you . . . But as I was saying, it has quite gone. Where it should be, there, on the left hand of the iconostasis, all is bare."

"Taken during the—the madness?"

"Surely."

"Not into safe keeping?"

"No. I asked Father Marcion. He is quite troubled, of course. The archangel's gate, you know, was the recourse of all those who wanted some help in getting into heaven."

"Then I can quite see why you went so often dear."

"You pay me a greater compliment than you know. Because San Gabriel's intercession worked, you see, only for those who might be said to be standing tip-toe on the portals of paradise, but needed some special grace to get inside. You should see all the glum and solemn faces there now, staring at the blank space. But hush, we are observed . . . "

There was a courteous inclination of the dark officer's sharp head, and the emblem at his collar caught the rays of light from the cracked chandelier. Both Countesses nodded gracefully back and applied their lorgnettes in unison. Within the dim, smeared lens of each they caught a glimpse only of the heraldic device he wore. It seemed to them to represent a crowned, winged snake.

That night, in the early hours, the revolutionary underground succeeded in causing an explosive blast on one of the busiest boulevards. The soldiers from the International Commission lined up the dead, or what could be found of the dead, on trestles under canvas in the park. Those who thought they might have lost someone in the attack were permitted to see if they could identify them. The news reached even the narrow inlet where the Dutch houses were: and "Meinheer" Kournos, shouldering a heavy satchel, made his way there in the early dawn. As he bent to look at each face or form, he secreted a sacred splinter from his bag within their ragged remains. He could not think what else to do.

But he was not the only one with an idea of this kind. For on the pavements and steps that led to the busiest churches, certain sellers would step out from the railing or the lime trees where they had been leaning. "Old Mother! Here is a piece of the Mother of All Mercy—won't you look after her? Only a few kopeks. A sure route to good fortune, and a sure protection too." Some piece of painted wood, provenance uncertain, would every so often change hands, and the old woman would secrete her purchase in her apron, saying a speedy prayer.

IV. Around the Dutch Stove

As he now had no firewood, Mr. Kournos asked his friend of the first Dutch house, the scholar Dr. Cornelius, very possibly descended (it was thought) from one of the great Tsar's original Dutch advisers, if he might join him that evening around the stove; and as was the custom, they invited the other two occupants of the houses. After tea had been dispensed from the hissing silver urn, and sipped in a suitable thoughtful silence, the old trader began haltingly to explain why he had no kindling to warm him, and to warn the others to be careful about what they bought. He soon found, though he had not quite intended to, that he must tell the whole story of his strange visitor: and they all listened very intently.

It was their habit to defer to the retired ballerina first in the making of remarks. And Madame Helena did not disappoint them. In her very precise tones, as clear and pointed as she kept her toes, fingers and eyebrows, in memory of her time on the stage, she said:

"My friends, the city is full of strangers. I was invited to tea with the Countess Tamara today. She was such an admirer of my work formerly you know, and she has not forgotten. She loves to remember some of the wonderful performances we gave, even though it was so long ago, and I am now—as you find me. Not, gentlemen, that I could wish for any nobler company, but—you understand . . . ? Now, the Countess—we are on first name terms, you will well believe, but still I cannot quite bring myself to omit her title—well she, it seems, was quite transfixed by a young officer at some reception or other she had attended. Well, strictly between us, there is nothing unusual about that, now that better times are upon us: but it was not quite that kind of aesthetical pleasure that had captivated her. Why do I mention all this? Ah, yes, yes. You see, Mr. Kournos, all she could remember of the soldier was how utterly black everything about him was, just as you described your visitor. Do you suppose they might be from the same power?"

Mr. Kournos nodded politely, and ran his fingers through his white beard.

Unusually, it was the boatman who spoke next.

"If it is so, friends, they have agents everywhere. You know that I take barrels and crates from the city to the outer islands and back. It is dull work. Sometimes I have to seek shelter in a tavern or café there, though they are mean and dingy places enough. It is just, you will see, there is nowhere else for an old sculler like me to find a welcome. The one I was in today was full of a muttering about some young woman who had visited, a mysterious young lady she certainly was; and indeed all in black. She asked a lot of questions, they said."

There was a pause while the host at their gathering replenished their tea glasses and offered small plates of preserved vegetables.

The old dancer jerked her head up suddenly, displacing a little cloud of rouge and powder. "I have just remembered one thing more that dear Tamara—the Countess, you know—confided in me. This soldier showed a very keen interest in a conversation she was having about a miracle-working relic, that vanished during the, during the—" (what was the word the Countess always employed?)—"madness, shall we say. It was the one they call the gate of the archangel. Yes, Saint Gabriel lighting the way to heaven, you see."

The others knew that Dr. Cornelius was a scholar, but they would have been hard pressed to say exactly what he studied.

His North Sea ancestry, if that is what it was, might still be discerned in a lineage of fair hair, now more a tarnished gold, and eyes flecked with blue and green. He wore an English tweed suit, now very threadbare and reinforced with leather, and a loose knitted tie.

"That's rather interesting, Madame. They say there are relic-collectors amongst the international staffs, even though some of them are Lutherans or even heathens. Indeed, I may tell you all, what I could not say quite so openly in former days, this: that all angels are gods disguised. You see in Gabriel he who is really, if we look into our older faiths, Aurionis, the spirit of the north-east wind. When I tell you that this was the god the pagans trusted to steer them into paradise through the stars, you will soon see that Gabriel and he are one. It is perfectly possible that beneath that painted panel—what did you call it, Madame?—the door of the archangel? Door? Gate? Beneath that there was once an image of the older spirit. I have studied these legends for many years, and I am almost sure of it."

There was a chorus of gratifying surprise at this pronouncement. But after a short silence, Mr. Kournos asked: "Do you think, then, is it possible, that these strangers might be followers of the old god? Anything is possible in these times."

Dr. Cornelius shook his head of gold and black hair. "No, that is hardly likely. Of course, there are esotericists with such interests, but I believe they are few and for the most part unadventurous. Besides, since they seemed to adore the colour black so much, these officials, whatever they are, would be more likely to serve . . . " he trailed off as a troubled thought seemed to toll deep in the belfry of his mind.

"Yes, Doctor? To serve . . . ?" the old trader prompted.

"To serve . . . the dark."

"You mean . . . ?"

Madame Helena set her glass of tea and little china plate of morsels down with a clatter. "Doctor, one thing more the Countess told me, one thing more. This will bear you out. That soldier had an emblem at his collar, in obsidian and silver she said: and do you know what it was? Why . . . "

And she summoned up the image of the crowned and winged serpent.

The scholar of ancient myths became very grave. "Well, I hardly need to tell you, friends, what is the significance of that. One of the very oldest symbols. The sign of the Adversary. And he too had his precursor in the days before the saints were here, but the name that he had then is not known."

"Friends," Madame Helena said solemnly, "You would hardly call me devout, I am sure. But I do not feel that we four, who have become possessed of such a secret, can do nothing. Surely we must seek out these emissaries from 'a certain Power', find out whom they serve, and defy their purpose. What possible good could they want with the gate of the archangel? Surely, surely, they plan to slam the door to heaven shut!"

The scholar, the boatman and last of all the old trader, who had, after all looked into the eyes of 'the black lion', all nodded slowly.

The following afternoon, as they had arranged, the four gathered again to share what they had learnt from a morning of discreet but persistent questioning among their contacts. The gossip and speculations, the hints and glimpses, they had each garnered, Madame Helena from her artistic circles and aristocratic patrons, the boatman among the bargees and longshoremen, Mr. Kournos following the delicate filaments of his former web of trading and dealing associates, and Dr. Cornelius through the ruminations of fellow scholars and delvers in curious learning, all these meshed to form a single sign.

23

"M. Zalmuth has returned to his ruined Livonian watchtower on the promontory called The Fox's Muzzle," pronounced the old ballerina, "And he is inviting selected guests to visit him. There seems to be a soirée of sorts tonight."

"He was banished," added Dr. Cornelius, "after he published his *Book of Spells*: the Procurator of the Church had it banned and persuaded the authorities to send him away. It was a compendium of riddles, curses, incantations and oaths, all from our oldest religions, and from the Karelians especially. I knew him, somewhat, for he sought my advice on some translations from the old tongue, and some sources for his book. He is an aphorist, and a poet. And, I should say, a dilettante. He might very well be mixed up in this matter."

"Yes: he went to Paris, where they say he sulked and raged against the injustice of his exile," explained Madame Helena, "And presented himself to the French as a friend of liberty, persecuted. So they let him attach himself to the French Mission when it came here, and he is, it is said, under their protection."

"His is a name that kept recurring when I asked around my friends in clandestine commerce about who would be interested in old holy relics," confirmed "Meinheer" Kournos, "Not, you understand, that I myself ever traded in unofficial wares, certainly not; but of course one encountered such people."

The boatman had remained stolidly silent during these reports, but with a glint of a grin behind the clay pipe gripped in his jaws.

"Friends," he at last put in, "I too asked around about who was buying, who has money. This Zalmuth is a very wealthy man. He sends for every luxury and there is a daily vessel to his headland from the wharves. For example, it includes the choicest fruits from Astrakhan and even beyond, despite the fighting there. He has peaches, figs, apricots, grapes delivered to him, all preserved in snow."

The four contemplated such unheard of extravagance. But the boatman had not finished.

"So, I know the cargo man. And one thing he said made me suspicious. You would hardly believe, he said, how sensitive this boss is about the handling of the crates. Doesn't want the fruit bruised, I suppose. But they all have to be very carefully unloaded. You'd think, he said, they were full of precious treasures."

The flames in the Dutch stove crackled and the four considered all they had heard, in a careful silence. Beyond the walls of the old rose-brick house, of the stained and mildewed but still old, proud and distinctive house, the lapping of the dark waters of the great river could just be heard.

"Anyway," concluded the boatman, in an artfully offhand way, "He'll be glad of a day off. I'm taking his place tonight. Who wants to come with me? But before you agree: one thing more. As I talked to him, I am sure I saw, in the shadows, that woman they said came to the bar on the outer island. There was her face; her cap; her figure, all in black. If it is so, they are on to us, my friends."

A silence. Then:

"It should be me," said the scholar, "I can presume on my slight acquaintance with Zalmuth as an excuse for visiting, if it should be needed."

The old trader looked relieved. And Madame Helena said: "I shall light a candle for you."

V. A Taste of Pomegranates

It was very late when the boatman returned, clanging the corroded bronze bells at two of the Dutch houses with a desperate urgency. He was alone. In the delicately decorated room at Madame Helena's house, with its painted dolls, ballet shoes, photographs of admirers, little vase of faded silk flowers, and amber taper in a worn, polished golden candlestick, the boatman looked like a gnome who has strayed into a fairy court; and his face was as grim and gnarled and puzzled. Mr. Kournos tried to revive the dying fire in the stove but its warmth fell far short of the huddled trio. In the cold and the dimness they listened.

At first all the boatman could do was repeat a few phrases. "They have taken him. And the painting. I do not know where. I could not save him. A darkness fell upon me. I could not move. He has gone. Yes, it was in a wherry. It's not a boat I've ever seen on these waters. Three big triangular sails. Black. How fast it went. The wind was not so high. What drove the sails? I cannot understand."

Slowly, patiently, they persuaded him to explain more.

"Who has got him? Zalmuth? We can get the authorities . . . "

"Useless. Not him. No. The strangers."

"They are working for him?"

"No, no: not in the least. Their shadow fell upon him too."

"And where have they gone?"

"I do not know: I cannot say; they took to the sea . . . Yes, but back to the city: they were heading landward, up the estuary. Such a strange vessel. I never saw it before . . . . "

"You saw—the picture? The holy picture?"

The boatman stared at them, and slowly nodded; the question seemed to release his tongue.

"Certainly, certainly. Saw it? Ha, I handled it. Do you know how? How does Zalmuth smuggle out the images of the saints and angels from the city, under the eyes of the church and the internationals and the other privateers, eh? How does he do it? Very simple. In those crates of fruit, you see? First the fruit, then a board, then a silk lining, then the treasure, then the bottom of the crate. Conceal one treasure beneath another, see? Flaunt one extravagance, then who suspects another? Do you know what he did? We were late running in—the boat didn't handle like mine, and I had to negotiate the shoals. He and a page met us at the jetty and hurried us up the cliff path to his old citadel. He said he was 'charmed' to see the Doctor, but he wasted no time in greetings. A funny customer, this Zalmuth. Tall, wearing a big black cloak and a wide-brimmed hat, and on his fingers many rings that sent out bright rays . . . "

The boatman stopped and interrupted himself as a new thought came to him. "But where could *their* boat have been? It wasn't at the landing-place. There must be a hidden harbour nearby."

"The Fox's Muzzle," said Mr. Kournos, "has long been a place for contraband, so I understand. I am sure there will be places where boats could put in, unseen. They say when the Livonian knights had it they made secret stairways and passages too, in case they needed to escape from the pagans quickly. It is said the headland is riddled with them."

"Is that so? Well, he took us into the great hall. A big stone chamber. There are no windows, except tall narrow slits high up. He had huge torches flaming on the walls in iron brackets. But they didn't seem to cast light so much as shadow and as they sputtered and spat, it seemed the shadows leapt. It reminded me of the way the waves surge when the sea is sombre and angry. A feast was in progress and his guests were gathered around an old, bowed table: I never saw such food on there for a long time. Dr. Cornelius said he knew some of them."

Madame Helena leant forward. "Who were they? It might be important."

The boatman just shook his head. "Oh, poets, artists, prophets, I suppose," he said, "I never meet such sorts on the river, but I could believe it. Many of them were pale and—well, furtive. Lots of longhairs and suchlike. I'll bet some were there for the food. Who could blame them?"

"Zalmuth," he resumed, "had the page he keeps there—a youth all in black velveteen, with a faint moustache, poor lad—he had him carry around with great ceremony a particular delicacy I had carried over in the boat. It was a crate of pomegranates. I don't mind saying I stole one on the way over but I didn't reckon much to it. Like sucking perfumed water it was, with bits of slimy grit in, and the rind wasn't up to much either: sour. So I spat it out. Anyway, he had these offered to all his guests, and one by one, the crate emptied out. The Doctor had one too, poor soul. As if that were not enough, Zalmuth recited a poem he'd written on the subject of pomegranates. It went on a bit. And then, when they were all quite sated, and he had finished declaiming: *zut!*—just like some stage conjurer's trick. He flourished the crate, reached inside, took out the board, turned the box to face them all, unveiled the silk—and beneath—there it is, the gate of the Archangel. All gleaming gold and scarlet and unharmed as far as I could tell. And oh, how they all gasped, and the two of us included. I made as if to dart forward, but the Doctor held me back.

"'Gentlemen,' says Zalmuth, 'even the unholy and shunned like us, even those they cast out, we have our ticket to the stars, our passport to heaven. Saint Gabriel's sacred intercession! The herald of the gods! Here is our shining obol for the journey beyond. It is for us, and no-one else. The shunned shall be the elect!' And a lot more of the same."

"What I noticed next," the boatman resumed, "was how, among all the commotion—they were leaping up, striking the table, crowding around him, and making mock homage to the archangel—well, among all this, you see, the torch-flames writhed a lot more and the shadows with them, and all the shadows of Zalmuth's guests, cast against the stone walls, didn't seem quite right; didn't seem attached to them; were a bit wrong, awry. But of course that could just be what I thought I saw. Anyway, with all this hubbub, they didn't at first see when some other shadows detached themselves from the walls and came into the hall. And I saw three strangers enter there; all dark they were, darker still than the shadows, and not much doubt to us two who they were; the 'black lion', the young woman who came to the tavern, and the soldier of 'a certain power'."

Here the boatman stopped, ran his fingers around the blue kerchief at his neck, and fumbled for his clay pipe. With a gentle, quiet grace, the old dancer rose from her chair, took up the candle in its golden column, and placed this by the window that gave out onto the street, where it flickered in a shiver of draught. Then Mr. Kournos tried once more to stir the grey embers of the stove fire into flame.

"I think they only said one thing, and that was to Dr. Cornelius. 'Take that up and come with us.' Yes, that was it: and that was all. And all the others were staring at them, and in the twisting of the torchlight I caught sight of the emblem that each of three wore; in silver and black, the serpent, crowned and winged. And so, I think, did these others: for they shrank back. Of course, Zalmuth was astounded, and he rushed forward and shouted, 'You shall not have it', or something like that. He thought they were from the church or the occupiers, I suppose. But he soon discovered his mistake. You see, they just turned to him and stared. And, whether he then saw the sign, and dimly understood, or could not stand their stares, or both, I do not know: but he subsided very feebly."

Mr. Kournos, remembering, said; "The darkness fell upon him."

There was a long pause. The boatman gripped the glowing white bowl of his clay pipe and drew in deeply from its stem. Pale tendrils floated upwards.

"And upon me," he said, simply. "I pursued them as they took him, but they turned as they descended the stone steps and looked hard at me. And then I found I could not go on. By the time I recovered and got down to the shore, all I could see was that black-sailed boat, out to sea: not much doubt about who was on it. But the wind was not so high; what drove it so far, so fast? And where have they taken him?"

The embers shifted in the stove; and the flame of the golden candle wavered.

VI. A Scholar of Dualism

The boat with the vast dark sails drew into the shore; the city rose before it. The scholar, holding the sacred picture re-adorned in its golden silk, scanned the scene hungrily, looking for landmarks. But the night and the mist hung over the city and he saw only the faintest image of the domes and towers, the orbs and pinnacles, the great stone-ringed fingers that he knew, or hoped, must still be raising their signs of salvation and adoration to the sky. There were lights: but they were dimmed lights, subdued by the darkness and fog, like the moon when the clouds are upon it.

At the quayside, a carriage waited; a black brougham, gleaming, with two horses reined-in by a hunched-up jarvie at its helm. The neck and flanks of the horses shone, as if they had been meticulously groomed; and they were both dappled greys. The captive scholar had time to admire the fine admingling of their coats, pale as dawn and veiled as dusk, the way the white and grey blended and blurred. Quaintly, the young woman in the peaked cap and rough tunic helped him in, as he unsteadily tried to preserve the picture and his balance together. All four took their seats; the hood and the doors were closed; and the horses took them away at a brisk trot. Dr. Cornelius regarded each of the three strangers in turn. No word had been said in the voyage from the citadel: now he thought he would try again.

Addressing the long-maned figure in the black cloak, he said:

"You are a collector?"

A dark shining gaze: but silence . . . His companions stirred: they seemed amused.

"Our task is nearly done," the young woman said, in her gentle murmur, "What harm can it do? Tell him."

The "black lion" raised his head proudly. "Yes. I collect—souls."

Dr. Cornelius knew that he had somehow half-expected this reply. He decided a studied insouciance might not go amiss.

"Mine?"

"We shall see."

The reply was not exactly comforting: but neither was it quite as conclusive as it could have been. The scholar thought he would try his luck further. Turning to the slender, short-haired young woman, he asked:

"And you? You told the workmen you were an enlightener?"

Her pale features assumed a slight smile. "All souls find enlightenment at last: even in the dark."

"Even mine?"

This time there was no equivocation. "Even yours."

The soldier interrupted, perhaps not wanting to be left out. "They called me a liberator. And so I am." And he turned his gaze to the scholar; and in his eyes, around the radiant black irises, there seemed to Dr. Cornelius to be a cruel shape, a curved and gleaming blade of light. He clung to the painting with a tighter grip.

The carriage jolted gently through the streets. Dr. Cornelius tried to listen for any changes to the sound or the stepping of the horses, as from cobbles to paving, or from levels to slopes; but they seemed to proceed with the same even pace over all the terrain. The blinds were drawn and he could not see out: he tried to imagine the streets they were traversing, and he realised for the first time how much he, though often a recluse crouched over his books, still loved the city where he sometimes walked. He found he did not think of the grand buildings now, but of the little places he knew; a café where the schnapps was good and came with a faint bitter-orange flavour; a bookshop with a creaking door and pamphlets strewn upon the floor; the Grand Orient Humidor, where he got his pipe tobacco, and men he knew to nod to gathered around the stove to try the latest imports, and talk of nothing much, amiably, for hours; the pen-and-ink shop where he bought the simple instruments of his craft, and they had that old imperial quarto paper in a reassuring tint of amber. All through the riots and the uprisings and the insurrections and the restorations, under old and new masters, these had somehow contrived to stay open, or as open as they ever were, at the whim of their keepers. Suddenly, these things were very precious to him, small, shabby and flawed though they were; and he knew he could not bear to travel much longer in the carriage with these strangers from "a certain power", these interlopers in his city.

The steady rhythm of the dappled horses soothed him, despite his longing and the keen edge of trepidation that curved around him, and he found himself drifting into a half-sleep. He thought of the stout old "Meinheer", trader Kournos; of the boatman, who had run after them and tried to stop them from taking him, until they turned on him; and of Madame Helena, and her harmless little vanities and preciousness; and he remembered with a smile, even in this drifting dream, how she had said she would light a candle for them. He tried to picture that faint light in her own, so well-adorned, Dutch house, one of four; he saw her face, and the face of his other friends, in the half-light it would cast. And then there was a jolt, and, in his reverie, he murmured that they must be careful, or the light would go out.

The door of the carriage opened silently and coldness came in. The soldier stood outside and gestured to him with a slight bow to get out. Without being asked, he took up the picture and held it to him. The "liberator" led the way, and the "collector" and the "enlightener" walked behind him, closely. Like a funeral procession, he suddenly thought, with a deep lurch of misgiving inside him; and these, my only mourners. He heard the carriage pull away: so, there was to be no return journey, then? The night air was hard; and fog still pervaded the city. He could see only a few steps in front of him, treading carefully alongside his dark escorts. They did not march very far, but came upon an arched wooden door. A sudden gust of wind rose and clanged the shining bell. Again: and a third time. There was movement within. The door opened slightly. A grave, grey-bearded face regarded them. Dr. Cornelius stared at him with a strange surge of hope and despair. A priest! Why had they brought him to a priest?

The officer leaned forward and said: "This is yours." And he jerked his head with an impatient gesture at the holy treasure the scholar carried. The priest opened the door wider and considered the three dark figures. Then he gazed at the scholar. "I am Father Marcion," he said. "What is it you have returned?"

Dr. Cornelius removed the golden silk and held the gate of the archangel up to the eyes of the priest, who bowed his head, and gently took the mystic picture from the white fingers of his visitor. Then he said a few words of blessing over the scholar's head. The narrow light from the arched doorway of his house did not reach as far as the three who had brought Dr. Cornelius here; and the priest strained his sight to make them out more clearly.

"And you—shall I offer you the church's blessing too?"

There was a sudden burst of laughter; and the priest drew back.

The soldier leant his sleek head towards him, so that the priest could see his eyes, and the emblem that he wore at his neck.

Father Marcion was not to be cowed a second time. "I know you, then. And what have you done with the image of Saint Gabriel? What can you have done?"

"Don't worry. We haven't so much as touched it."

"Then why have you restored this to us, knowing that through its power many will be saved from your—your *master*?"

The soldier shook his head. "His ways are legion and not to be questioned, as surely you must know. But," (more suavely), "trouble yourself with these two riddles in your twilight days. Firstly, why would *our* Master want what belongs to you? What glory and power can they bring Him? And—oh, let this trouble your faith as it once troubled mine, why not?"

The young woman touched his arm in restraint. Almost tenderly, he returned the touch, in reassurance.

"Sometimes, haven't you seen, there is a strange complicity between our two Commanders in the ordering of the world? And that is as unfathomable as our darkness and as inscrutable as your light, priest."

Father Marcion did not respond by the slightest movement of his solemn brow or slightly haughty eyes.

"Go from here," he said.

The officer bowed, in mock courtesy. "It has been an interesting mission. When the light fails, shadows leap up; and when it is steadied, they return to their hollows. So—*adieu*, or, perhaps, *au revoir*." And with a flourish the three were gone into the darkness.

The researches of Dr. Cornelius these days have turned towards the history and mythology of dualism, and perhaps no man has studied these more deeply. Yet the source and inspiration of his work he has shared with only a few: three friends, to be exact. After the passage of some months, he was even able to make light of his experiences upon the black vessel, in the carriage drawn by dappled horses, and in that silent procession he had thought might be his last.

Indeed, he has formed a theory.

Dr. Cornelius says: "I do believe that their master had grown tired of the entreaties of those mild souls who had lost their way to paradise without the archangel's light to guide them, and who had cast up instead at the gates of Hades. Can you imagine? So he sent his emissaries to restore the old order. As in the city, so in the empyrean."

The Dawn at Tzern

When they brought the news to Postmaster Conrad, he was sitting in the last of the sun in the late afternoon of that winter's day, on the old larchwood bench in front of the low, white-walled village post office. His gaze did not seem to shift from the distant deep blue mountains to the West. So the forest messenger had to repeat what he had said, and then express it in ever more simple ways, using the terms of endearment the country people had.

"The Emperor is dead. The King and Emperor is dead. Great Uncle Frank, yes? Old Joey? He has gone."

Slowly, Postmaster Conrad nodded: and that was all the satisfaction the messenger had for his remarkable news. He strode on to find some more gratifying listener. After some moments alone again, the Postmaster rose slowly to his feet, and bowed his head briefly—but whether to the mountains, the setting sun, or the memory of the dead Emperor, he could not himself have said. Then he trod carefully over the stone step into his post office. There he conducted the careful stock check that he was always obliged to do at the end of each day of opening. He found that he had precisely two hundred and twenty seven stamps, each with the old Emperor's effigy upon them, solemn, bald and luxuriously whiskered. He was tinted in plum for the stamps of the common letter post, royal blue for the express service, and evergreen for parcels.

Soon his image would no doubt be replaced. Who was the heir now? Would they let there be an heir? He had heard from the hotheads some talk that the world had no need of emperors and kings, that the people should rule instead. He did not understand such nonsense. How could you fit "the people" upon a stamp? They could never tell him that.

Postmaster Conrad drew himself up in his uniform of midnight blue, with its glinting brass buttons and badges, like so many bright lights in the night sky. The one that shone the most of all was in recognition of his forty years service, almost as long (if the thought were permissible) as the Emperor himself, whom he had now outlived. He took a yellow duster and thoughtfully wiped the ink stamp bearing the seal and inscription of his office, and the name of the village in stark, heavy characters; TZERN. Then he locked away his stock and instruments in the small black iron safe, which was impressed with the mark of the imperial double-eagle, and pulled down the wooden shutter.

He stood in the doorway with his keys held loosely. The light was dim now and the far mountains dark. Over to the East the distant lights of the provincial city could just be seen, like the glinting gold eyes of a pack of beasts in their lair. Somewhere out there, he reflected, over the mountains or the city, the soul of the old Emperor was finding its way—but on what journey, to what destination? He remembered reading in the almanac that the fiery voyage of a great comet accompanied the passing of the English King Edward. And he was a parvenu by comparison. What starry portent, then, would mark the much greater transition of the Emperor? His gaze, still keen, quartered the skies. No sudden blaze was to be seen. They were beginning to be strewn with the illuminated seed of the heavenly fields, but no great fiery bloom burst among them. Why might this be? He sighed, stroked his own neat white moustaches, and pondered. Could the Emperor's spirit, indeed, wholly abandon the country where his mortal form had reigned for so very long? Surely it would stay, might even stand ready to return one day, like they said of Barbarossa, Sobieski, El Cid and other great men. Might it not seek out some quiet, forgotten corner of that great realm for its time of peace and repose? Old Conrad nodded to himself again, and then turned and pulled the stout timbers of the door sharply into place, fastening the locks with his silver keys. Then, a resolution quietly forming, he walked slowly to his home.

The image of the new Emperor-and-King arrived in long perforated sheets some weeks later, inside an official manilla wallet. Postmaster Conrad carefully broke the black wax seal and counted out what had been sent. Then he looked thoughtfully at the portrait. It showed a young man, a very young man, with the merest hint of a moustache, and a troubled, anxious look in his eyes. The old official shook his head sorrowfully. That was not a man born to bear the burden of Empire, he was sure of it. And it was only, he knew, by the most unexpected sequence of events that this young King Karl (he could not quite bring himself to apply the grander imperial title) had come to the throne at all. Maximillian, the Emperor's brother, murdered by brigands in Mexico: Crown Prince Rudolf, a victim of some strange conspiracy at Meyerling; Franz Ferdinand assassinated by rebellious Slavs.

He read the instructions in the dark script on thick yellow paper, telling him to destroy all stocks of the old stamps bearing the dead Emperor's head, and from now on to use only these depicting the new heir. He took out the old stocks and placed them on the counter, side by side with the new, then looked from one to the other. It was like comparing some great old god with a nervous young acolyte. Then he sighed, and ran his gnarled forefinger along either side of his whiskers. He knew it would not do. He knew he could not do it. For the first time in a dutiful and distinguished career, Postmaster Conrad would have to disobey an order. He reflected on the consequences. In this village of four hundred souls, and few visitors, there were not many letter-writers and hardly any who would give much thought to the stamps he issued to them, at least for a few weeks. And the ranks of the officials were so depleted, that it would perhaps be a long time before anyone further afield noticed, if they ever did. So his mind was quite made up: here in the community of Tzern, things would go on as they had before; there would be no change in the ordering of things; the Emperor would still preside over his post. If the imperial soul were indeed searching for a place to find its repose and await some distant summoning, there would be a sign here that he was not forgotten. Thoughtfully, he locked away the new stamps bearing the head of the melancholy young impostor.

Then Postmaster Conrad stepped outside his post office and gazed at the village below. The tall, deep spire of the wooden church, the little bell-tower of the school, the many modest but well-kept houses with their painted shutters and steep-sloping roofs, the thin spirals of pale blue smoke issuing from a few hundred twisted chimney-pots: all was as it had been for much of his lifetime here. The foothills ran in green domes almost to the doors of the outlying cottages, and they rang with the dull, gentle, reassuring tolling of the bells tied to the necks of the tough goats and rugged sheep that grazed there. Gashes of glittering white denoted where the streams fell, and their very distant rush could also just be discerned, like the soothing murmur of an old lullaby, in the village air. The old official gazed at all this and heard, as with an inward sense, those immemorial sounds: it seemed as if they ran within him like the sap in a great tree.

For many days his simple scheme of prolonged loyalty to the late Emperor-and-King proceeded without a hitch. As he expected, none of the villagers noticed that the new stamps were not in use yet at his office; indeed, they probably gave the matter no thought at all. His stock did not diminish very much. Moreover, the portrait of the monarch that hung in the school in its carved oak frame had not been taken down, and the sepia photogravure of the familiar figure in hunting costume, which hung in the Great Boar Inn, below the smoke-blackened beams and above the marred, bowed, but polished trestle tables, also remained in place. There was nothing here that could cause the soul of the old potentate to pause, were it to wander in the streets of Tzern. More and more, Postmaster Conrad reasoned to himself that this was the very refuge such a great and (it must be) wearied spirit must seek, when at last it came to rest from its first celestial obligations, whatever they might be. He had started a careful conversation with the village priest, to see what he might think.

Father Serafino had a silver head of unruly hair that looked as though it was aspiring to become a halo, when the time was right, and it gave an unexpectedly holy aura to his otherwise rather sardonic, narrow, dark-eyebrowed visage, which nearly always bore in its worm-coloured lips (except when actually conducting the sacred offices) a thin cigarette of Latakia tobacco. He had come to the village seven years ago, and it was whispered by cobbler Matthias, that ardent sceptic, that the priest, who seemed too learned and aloof for so modest a charge of souls, had been sent to this remote duty for some obscure misdemeanour against the principles of the Church. Conrad found the curé outside the café, watching his parishioners pass by with an unenchanted eye, occasionally consulting his breviary, or at any rate a book that might be assumed to be a breviary, and sipping at treacle-black coffee. He briefly nodded as the postmaster took a place beside him.

His visitor decided to be frank. "They have sent me the stamps of the new king."

The priest's watchful face merely registered a slight rise of the left eyebrow at this perhaps not entirely extraordinary news.

"It seems too soon. Unseemly. The soul of the old Emperor can barely be still yet."

Father Serafino exhaled a cloud of violet-tinted fumes from the censer of his jaw, and regarded the postmaster with slightly more interest.

"You think he will be restless?"

A shrug. "So great a man . . . "

Two yellowing fingers clutching the burning taper of precious tobacco wagged at him

"Great or small, we all come to the footstool of the gods at last."

"Of God, you mean?"

Father Serafino eyed him, then smiled. "No doubt."

"Anyway, Father, I have decided not to use them—just yet."

The dark padre yawned, and a silver ring of intertwined serpents glinted on a surprisingly delicate little finger. "Until you have used up the others. Very proper —and, *ahm*, thrifty."

"Oh no, oh no. They told me to put them into use straightaway, and destroy the others. But I find that I cannot. Here the Emperor will not be so lightly cast aside. That is what I say."

"That is very loyal of you, Conrad. Won't it spell trouble?"

"*Pfuff!* Who is to know?"

The priest regarded him solemnly. "Indeed. My own lips are sealed." And he twisted those narrow vermicular strips as if to demonstrate this, or perhaps in some half-suppressed secret smile.

"After all, there must be some place in the Empire where his soul can find a welcome."

Father Serafino may have decided to humour the pious postmaster in his theologically unorthodox assertion, for he simply nodded and added, "Yes, I see. Where the old eagle can come to rest."

His visitor nodded vigorously. Ah, the advantages of learning: for that was exactly the right image for what he had in mind. A great and ancient imperial eagle, descending at last from the wide skies to find a hidden eyrie.

As he retraced his steps back to the little white post office, the shoemaker called out to him from his narrow shed of a shop: "Why are you talking to that old rook? Don't waste your time. All such will soon be made to work!" The lean, bald-headed artisan was a confirmed conspirator for the reign of the working man. Postmaster Conrad poked his head through the half-door: "Cobbler Matthias," he said, pointing to the shoe he was repairing, "hold your tongue and mend your soul!"

After some further sips at his dank coffee, Father Serafino repaired to the bare study of his presbytery, which stood to one side of the wooden church. This room contained a rough-hewn desk and a reed-woven chair; a black wooden crucifix pinned to the wall, which had contrived to tilt at a peculiar angle as if pointing toward the east, and a painted panel in faded hues of rose, gilt, indigo and saracen green. There were figures on the panel which might very well be holy, for there was a glimpse of upraised wing, of pure pale limbs, of a shining corona, and of coloured vestments that themselves seemed like plumes, as if from some Persian bird. The study also contained books, which were treated without ceremony, standing in towering ziggurats around the desk.

The priest had received a delivery of his favourite tobacco from Mr. Alamadda, a merchant of Upper Lebanon, sent via the consular post in the port of Latakia, which had somehow clung on in this outpost of the Ottoman Empire, and also still used the old Emperor's stamps (for it had probably been quite forgotten by the imperial postal authorities). The small parcel, like a worn golden scroll, had made its way across hazardous waters and unfriendly territory, as if under unexpected protection, to reach him here, so far away. He broke the black seal which bore the trade mark or emblem of Mr. Alamadda, somewhat blurred: it might suggest the tall leaves of a thriving plant, or tongues of flame, or outspread feathers. Any villager witnessing his attention to the contents of the packet would have been surprised, though. Knowing his ardour for the rich rank herb, they might have expected him to examine the roll of tobacco first: but this he did not do. He put it aside, and gave his attention with the utmost care and with a keen gaze to—the wrappings. These were of a deep yellow, and ragged at the edges, and they held writing. It was a writing in no characters that any of the villagers were likely to have seen, deeply scriven in black, with firm, sharp strokes, and with curious markings. Father Serafino gave himself to study this, his thin face watchful, like a jackal's. Tracing the text carefully, he enunciated a title: *The Book of the Winged Ones*. Then he continued murmuring.

If things had indeed gone on much as they always had before, it is possible that Postmaster Conrad's ploy would have continued for quite some time, long enough certainly for the Emperor's spirit, quartering his vast realm, to discern the candle of faithfulness glowing in this forgotten corner, and make a descent towards it, as his servant fervently trusted. The pouchy, bristling portrait of the aged monarch was still placed upon the thin yellow letters of Grandmother Esther to her daughter in the regional capital, where she was a dancer, or so it was said; upon the stucco-white weekly forms of the village clerk to the authorities; upon the schoolmaster's frequent letters to bookshops and learned journals; upon the cobbler's spikily-addressed short missives to distant radicals, carefully sealed with red wax, which the censors equally scrupulously undid and resealed; and upon the priest's correspondence on a fine amber paper with his superiors and, more frequently, with his tobacco trader in the Levant. All these would scarcely have altered very much his stock of the imperial stamps, though it must of course have gradually dwindled.

But one day in December as the roads were hard with hoar frost, and the poplars all mere skeletons of wood, there came to the village of Tzern four covered wagons drawn by lean sweating horses with white eyes. And from these there stumbled a score or more of men in grey battledress, torn and stained: and some wore bandages on their head or over their eyes, and others walked with the aid of makeshift crutches made out of rough poles or limbs of trees, and a few had an empty sleeve. A young officer, who looked to the postmaster's eyes rather like the youth they said was the new king, with a murmur of a moustache and quiet tired eyes, called out the clerk from his office with the parish insignia, and told him he must requisition houses for all his men and send the village doctor to them. They would be here several days to rest before they pressed on. A little later, this Lieutenant Weiss told old Conrad that (as they had lost their field post en route) he was obliged to take some of his stamps so that his men could write home, which they had been unable to do for many weeks, owing to the "conditions". He would issue an official receipt or whatever the postmaster liked, but stamps he must have.

The Postmaster paused, not out of any doubt as to the correctness of his course of action, but at a quandary about what to hand over. Should he take out the new stamps he had so long shunned, and thus risk offending the Emperor's spirit? Or should he offer so much from his precious reserve of the older stamps? The officer mistook his hesitation.

"Old fellow," he said, "my men have been in retreat—yes, in retreat I tell you, for days now, picked off one by one by partisans or brigands, who can tell the difference? We have ridden hard to find a place, however briefly, where we might not be harried. One of my men knew the way through the passes and defiles, to get us here. Now I must keep their morale up and stop them going off their heads or trying to desert. A letter to a sweetheart, or a mother, or a brother, or some elder man of their home place (like you)—that will help. Do you see?" And he looked wearily at him, while fingering his leather pistol holster.

Postmaster Conrad nodded, and made a gesture towards his cap, like a salute. Quickly he fetched the black ledger and withdrew several sheets of the Emperor's stamps. "The messenger comes at midday," he said, "and will take whatever mail is ready. Indeed, he may wait a little longer if someone buys him a plum-spirit or so . . . "

That night the Postmaster shone the brass buttons of his uniform with extra vigour, counted out his stock with deliberate care, pursing his lips, and stood outside scrutinising the sky in vain hope of seeing some sign of the approach of the Emperor's soul.

Father Serafino soon became foremost amongst the villagers in tending to the wounded soldiers. Of course, he could be expected to go at once to them to offer what spiritual consolation he might after their ordeals, though in the past his pastoral care had perhaps been more dutiful than ardent. But he worked tirelessly at assisting the doctor to tend wounds and fix splints to limbs, at offering the men drinks and cigarettes and books, at helping them write letters home: and he also simply listened to them, as they spoke of what they had witnessed at the front, and what had happened to their comrades. He was matched in this only by the shoemaker, who went amongst the men preaching sedition and the war's end.

To one youth in particular the priest gave tender attention. From what far-flung corner of the imperial domains he came, it was hard to say. His skin was a singular olive-green-gold colour, his face had high cheekbones and delicate figuring, his hair was very dark and his eyes quite black: and he said his name was Mishael. He was physically uninjured, but it was clear that his mind had been tilted awry. He would remain silent for long periods: and he would be found wandering around the village as if looking for something; and he would also spend time staring at the night sky.

The priest invited Lieutenant Weiss to the presbytery, offered him a glass of his treasured Black Chartreuse, and asked about the boy. The officer eyed his host quizzically. "I know little of his origins. I think he came perhaps from one of our enclaves in what they call Asia Minor. Certainly he is from no part of the Empire that I have ever seen. In any case, we are a mongrel pack and after this war it soon no longer matters where men come from. I do not think you can imagine, Father, what my men have undergone. And it would not be fair on your sleep, or even your faith perhaps, to say too much. We were at the front for fourteen nights without respite: there were no reserves, you see. Where we stood was a vile pool of mud and what was left of men. The bombardment was intense, relentless: the vast noise, the great bursts of light, the sudden eruption of soil and trees and the opening of smouldering craters where once there had been a station of soldiers: all that we witnessed day after day. And then the silence was in some ways even more awful. Well, it is hardly surprising if in such conditions men's minds play tricks upon them. This Mishael became convinced that he was invulnerable, you see. He would throw himself into the foremost raiding parties and most desperate sorties, and it is true he would always come back. Of course, to begin with, he was a sort of hero, and you may have seen the ribbons he wears. But after a while, as will happen, the men began to wonder aloud how he always returned, and sometimes he alone: and I think they rather feared him."

"Mind you," the lieutenant resumed, after a sip at the ancient spirit, "I have nothing against him whatever in the military sense. He did more than his duty. In any event, it soon emerged he was not exempt from the strain we were all under. For, just before we finally gave way and had to pull out, in very hazardous circumstances I may say, he came to me very calmly and said he knew that things would be well for our troop, that we would get away. I assumed he had gleaned some knowledge of the enemy's dispositions from his secret forays and asked him to say how he knew.

The young subaltern stroked his chin: and his eyes became dimmed. "'The Ziiz,'" he said to me, "'the Ziiz, the Ziiz.' That's how it was. All gibberish to me. He still stood there staring at me as if I should understand. At last he threw up his hands and said hoarsely, 'A *wundervogel*. As vast as the night itself. We are under its wings'."

The priest's dark eyebrows drew together. "Yes. A magical bird of the Hebrews."

Lieutenant Weiss put down his glass, regretfully. "I see. An old fairy tale from his childhood, it may be. A sad affair, you'll agree. Do what you can for him, Father. For all of us."

On the eve of Epiphany, Father Serafino was to be found consulting again the scroll that Mr. Alamadda had sent him from some source in the wastes of the Levant, some decaying hermitage or desert monastery perhaps. Once more, in his bare room, with the oddly oriented cross and the painted panel of high and aureoled figures, he murmured the words in an old tongue that were incised upon the golden leaves. The boy Mishael slept on a makeshift couch in one corner, his face graceful in repose and his limbs like those of a contented animal.

Meanwhile, Postmaster Conrad checked once again the last of his stock of the Emperor's stamps, a few of each: the deep damson of the common stamp, ultramarine blue for the express, and laurel-green for parcels. The colours, so familiar to him throughout the years of his service, seemed to take on themselves a character and cast their lustre upon the room.

The late dawn of the day of the Magi was heralded by a vast scarlet sunrise, a hot vibrant red that filled the horizon, edged with translucent gold and with tendrils of malachite green. It was accompanied by minarets and spires of faint rising smoke, ichors of smouldering indigo and columns of diffuse, roiling darkness, like molten basalt. Within this great, volcanic sunrise, it was possible to see strange forms and figurings limned against the light.

The old Postmaster, when he rose to the day, knew at once that the time had come. He who had seen so many dawns had never seen one so magnificent as this. Here for sure was the sign of the coming of the Emperor's soul, all arrayed in the colours of his paper sigils, his stamps. His eyes saw in the flaming tableau the outline of a dark soaring eagle making its solemn, majestic way from the east.

The olive-gold face and limbs of the youth Mishael seemed to draw upon themselves the far-flung glow of the aurora, so that he stood as one transfigured. In his black eyes there was impressed the image of a huge crowned bird, rising from the cresset of the day, and holding aloft its wings.

Father Serafino's silver hair seemed to glint, too, with the myriad hues of the horizon; it was as if a faint nimbus of the great scarlet, gold and purple ceremony played in paler tints about his head. The Latakia cigarette was absent from his mouth. His hand clutched the breviary, or whatever other book it was he held that might pass for a breviary. His lean face looked hard at the stormy dawn, noting the plumes of many colours that had formed there. And he said to himself: "It is the rising of the Peacock Angel."

Cobbler Matthias, who had been hard at work some hours already, spat a boot nail into the palm of his hand, and glared briefly out of the grimy window of his workshop. "The red dawn," he said to himself, "at last."

Lieutenant Weiss raised his field-glasses to his wan eyes. He saw a burning city. It was time to gather his men, and move on.

The Walled Garden
on the Bosphorus

The walled garden on the Bosphorus had a narrow blue door opening out onto the waterway, a few stone steps descending from this and, affixed to their side, an iron staple where a boat might be moored. Here was kept one of the one-man sailing boats used on the water, with their single sharp triangle of white cloth. At times, I later found, the boat would be taken out to lonely islands and harbours, for its pilot to talk to the fishermen, goatherds, inn-keepers and priests, and to explore the scattered stones of ruined temples and shrines that he heard about from them.

The garden itself was perhaps twenty paces long and rather less than that wide: a walnut tree dwelt in one corner and in another, a medlar with, in spring, its bright silver-green leaves and white flowers, and, in autumn its tight, tawny little fruits. Much of the garden was cobbled, and old moss grew between the cobbles. But there was also a minor rank meadow of wild grass and in this stood an ornate bench painted blue, and a round table on a single elegant stalk: its top was just big enough to accept a coffee tray. Around the bench there were overflowing pots of mint, tarragon and rosemary. A rectangular lead cistern held brackish black water: it was decorated with the dark head of an heraldic panther whose mouth held an arid iron spout

Glazed doors led from the garden into the modest single storey studio-house attached to it: the glass in the doors had a green tinge. The room beyond the doors was restful, with worn couches, octagonal inlaid side-tables, an ugly old black-and-gold ormolu clock, a brass coffee pot, an umbrella stand, possibly used more now for parasols or walking sticks, and made from a deep brown oak like the bindings on old leather books, a glass rose-water flask with a deep spout, and a few shallow blue ceramic dishes which were sometimes graced with rather dusty comfits.

Above the arched fireplace, on the stone of the chimney, there was an unusual picture. In a simple frame of thin black wood, preserved behind heavy glass, there was a sepia photograph. It showed a stretch of sea and then billowing illumined clouds rising above a city whose outline was now jagged and haphazard. In the lower left corner there was a caption in white text: it read, "The Doom of Smyrna". Turkish acquaintances who visited the owner of the picture noted this evidence of their re-taking of the city: but when Greek acquaintances called, they took it as a commemoration of their loss. The truth was that the owner simply admired the composition and drama of the piece, and the contrast between the eruption shown and the subdued, elegiac light. He liked, too, the epic resonance of the title it had been given, and it gave him cause, when he mulled over it in his studio, to reflect upon the "doom" that had come, or was yet to come, to other cities, or to men. Although its gunpowder mills had been bombed during the Great War, in its more recent history Constantinople had suffered none of the fire and destruction whose bloom the photograph had caught: it had become, indeed, a place of refuge. Its doom, perhaps, was a slower fate: the encroachment of twilight.

It was because of the refugees that I had come to the city. I had been sent to do work for the League of Nations. The former Ottoman capital had, since the Russian Civil War and the many minor wars that followed it, taken on the reluctant role of a kind of entrepot for fleeing humanity. Thousands were encamped in makeshift shelters on its margins or tried to burrow into its dense interior. The work of seeing to even the simplest of their needs was tiring and incessant. Yet even an international official is permitted some time to himself and it was while I was buying myself a tin of Marcovitch cigarettes one day that I chanced to meet the Frenchman who lived in the studio with the walled garden on the Bosphorus. He was waiting for a special order to be made up, and was willing to linger in talk. He gave himself the name of Felix Vrai—and I never knew any other—and we seemed to hit it off straightaway, as strangers sometimes will. It was rather as if we were resuming a friendship and a conversation that had happened before. I said as much during a brief lull in our talk, and Vrai seized upon the notion, saying certainly there would be those who believed in encounters in a previous, or different, existence. The remark interested me: and he could see that it interested me.

He invited me to accompany him to his quarters, which were not distant, and as we traversed the streets we passed the forlorn shells of the old pashas' palaces, which were grand but not vast, with deeply arched windows, unfurling rooflines and rusting gates, now drunken on their hinges. Cypress, Aleppo pine and juniper lingered in the wild gardens, in their mournful groves. The impression perhaps prompted Vrai to explain his presence in the city. He was studying, he said, the obscure faiths of the old Ottoman Empire. No belief, I gathered, no sect, was too curious to excite his interest, provided it was, or had been, or was reputed to have been, practised within the shimmering boundaries of the former trans-national state, the empire without a true Emperor, which had sprawled across the Levant, the Caucasus, the Balkans, and beyond, for so many centuries. The Druze did not escape him, nor the Alawwites, Maronites, Jacobites, Ismaili (those reputed descendants of the Assassins), nor the

Bogomils (peasant dualists), the half-pagan Huculs (mountain folk of the Carpathians, with their carved axes), nor the Sabbatians (who revered in secret a seventeenth century Jewish messiah), nor the Hasidim and their wise Zadiks, nor the last lingering lines of the Sephardi, who had come from Castile and Andalucia centuries ago under persecution, and ended in Salonika, nor even the Lipovanians (Ukrainians who were perhaps also pagans, or Old Believers, or both).

About all these, singly or in such groupings as suggested themselves, Vrai (as I afterwards saw) would compose essays reflecting upon their beliefs, not burdened by learned footnotes, not vitiated by scepticism, but written rather elliptically, in what I think of as the typically Gallic way. It was as if he were turning over in his fingers a carved gem, remarking upon how the light and the dark played upon each facet. He did not, of course, I soon learnt, attach himself to any of these beliefs: nor indeed, could it be said, to any belief.

Ensuring that I was comfortable in his shaded study, with a mint tea to one side and a little dish of walnuts-in-rosemary to the other, Felix Vrai spoke rather of what he saw, or glimpsed, than of what he thought. For all his studying of those rare and strange beliefs, it seemed to me that he found his own solace for the soul, such as it was, in the incidental encounters of the city. He said that when the moon shone upon the dark waters lapping below his gate, it would produce an uncanny sheen which sometimes made him shiver for a reason other than the chill of the night air, though he could not say what. He knew, too, that the streets of the abandoned capital (for the Kemelites had acclaimed Ankara, that dull provincial town, instead) held soft shadows that caused a certain pleasurable trepidation in him. His gaze was certainly drawn, he conceded, to the celebrated domes and minarets of the city, of course: yet he said that even a single bead of rainwater, iridescent upon a tram-wire, could cause him to stare in a kind of abstract wonder. All these things, he implied, gave him reason to consider afresh the stubborn mysteries of the world: but not to form any definite conclusions, still less to assert those to strangers, as the founders and followers of the faiths he studied had been moved to do. As he spoke of these things, though, his grey eyes glimmered and his lean form in its suit of twilight blue became tense and brittle.

When I called upon Vrai more often, eager to hear again his peculiar speculative conversation, I found out more, too, about his diurnal routine. Once a day, usually when the golden dusk was settling on the city like a fine pollen, he left his studio and went out to frequent the few shops he favoured. On a few rare occasions, I even accompanied him: and it was a joy to witness his little pleasures. There was a stationer where he never failed to find delight in the yellowing reams of octavo and folio paper; in the fat glass bottles of inks, shaded from *perle noir* through *gris nuage* to *bleu nuit* and then suddenly vivified by vials of scarlet, viridian and even Imperial purple; in the little printed wads of blotting paper bearing the stationer's name and crest; and especially in the jars of fine silver sand, for those ancients who still preferred to dry their writing in this way.

Second only to the stationer was the shop of sweetmeats, with its array of pastries flavoured with almonds, preserved lemon peel, Lebanese honey, Anatolian raisins, cardamom or even Zanzibar cloves. It was rare that Vrai did not permit himself to select a few of these.

Thirdmost, before the shops of more mundane wares must occupy his attention, there was the fragrant humidor of the old tobacconist Ghazan, where we had first met. Here he selected the precise and precious mingling for his personal blend, which would later be fed to his little amber-stemmed pipe and offered as an incense to the evening air, as he sat on the scrolled blue bench in his walled garden on the Bosphorus, and listened to the liquid ripples playing beyond his gate.

I say all this so that it will be discerned that Vrai, for all his recondite studies and speculations, was no ascetic, but loved the little pleasures of life, which made all the more mysterious for me, later, his sudden absence from them. Nor was he one of those scholars who are oblivious of their surroundings. Vrai did not fail to discern the signs of neglect and decay that lay about him as he made his way through the shadow-scented streets. On certain days, indeed, he once confided in me, they almost appealed to him more than the offerings of the shops he visited. It was as if, he said, another form of merchandise had been devised for him, one made of melancholy and dust, of hollowness and fallen hauteur: all these lost ruins of a vanished empire were for him to taste on the tongue of his imagination. If there were also mortal relics in the niches of the streets, he gave them coins and no further thought. But the tawny powder of crumbling stone, the stark green stalks of the ascendant weeds, the ochreous moss that clung to the unsteady roof-tiles, these preoccupied him sometimes, on his walks at dusk.

After we had met many times in the studio or in the walled garden, Felix Vrai explained to me, at first with hesitation, that there were three faiths, the rarest of all he had found in the former Ottoman domains, that troubled him the most, and which he had not yet been able to write about. With my permission, he said, pouring me out a rose-water cordial from his graceful glass vessel, he would like to tell me what he knew. These, he said, he had not been able to discover from his usual sources or from reference works, but had relied upon chance words and rumours, and the piecing-together of fragments of papyri. Soon, he would have to seek out more about them, if his study was to be complete: but he did not know how, or where. That the answer would come to him, though, he felt sure, for (if he did not put his trust in any particular beliefs), he had a certain sense of how fate fell. He allowed me then to take notes about what he said; indeed, I think he hoped I might do this. I have not added anything to them, and I do not advise anyone else to try.

Of all the sects he had heard about, he said, few whispers fascinated him as much as the suggestion that there existed still a clandestine following of the tenth century neo-Zoroastrian movement, the Qarmatians. Acting upon the conviction of the sovereign importance of the 1,500th anniversary of the death of the prophet Zarathustra, which was also coincident with a portentous conjunction of Saturn and Jupiter in the heavens, the Qarmatians had in those days sacked Mecca and captured the Black Stone, the Q'aaba. Under a young renegade Persian prince, they had revived the worship of fire, and used it to destroy many cities: and in his ninety-day rule, some said seventy, preparations were made for the return of the great Zoroastrian emanations. Whether they had indeed returned was now disputed. But the strongest assertion made by Qarmatian legend, in recounting these epochal events, was that, during its captivity the Black Stone had been pulverised, ground down, and its dark grains dispersed across the world so that Ahriman, the evil entity, would be confused by the holy veil now covering all things (the Stone miraculously recreated itself).

The safety of our world, the Qarmatians averred, depended upon this vast zaimph, like the veil upon the glory of the goddess Tanit, which safeguarded the city of Carthage. What we see now, therefore, is visible only through this sombre skein, this protective cloak: the true world in all its infinite splendour is richer far in its vivid colours and radiant light. Once it was understood, this myth explained much that was otherwise obscure, for example why the ancient poets, before the dark and sacred masking, were able to convey the world with more simple vigour; why Sappho saw brightness where Dante saw gloom.

And when he walked the streets of Constantinople, Felix Vrai said, he saw the justice of the Qarmatian belief: for everywhere wore a discernible skimming of black, a habit of decay. Even when the high sun searched out the city's innermost alcoves and arcades, the brass beams did not seem to disperse a certain kept veneer of shade. He supposed it might be the same in any city. It was possible, however, the most secret of the sect's writings suggested, to see beyond the dark chalking that lay upon the world, and behold it in its true brilliance; but such a step was fraught with danger, for it attracted the attention of Ahriman. So that when, as happened in rare revelations, he found himself contemplating a tree or stone or fountain made suddenly illuminate, there was always also a keen edge of trepidation, in case the brightness should bring a greater darkness in.

A second sect, still just possibly existing, that possessed his imagination at times, was that of the Archonites, founded by a heretic hermit in the deserts of Egypt. They held that God was indifferent to the fate of the world, which was the preserve of seven ranks of Archons, or demi-urges. These powers had but one sustenance: the souls of men; and it was their will to draw these to them by all the lures and vices of the world, each having charge of several of these. Only the untempted, such as an ascetic hermit, could avoid their greed and find a way through their avaricious ranks to the eternal. Vrai said that in piquant moments he would muse upon which particular of the Archons, who had all once been named, with their kingdoms, by this sect, had charge of (say) opium, or bhang, or the complex postures of the seraglio. Certainly, he thought that the city offered a fecund hunting-ground for the voracious Archons, and he could not claim to be free of the things that might excite their appetite.

There was a third arcane school of belief, Sethian perhaps in origin, but inflected by late Alexandrian Neo-Platonism, which held that, putting the point simply, "everything is also something else": that there is no being nor object upon the planet that does not have a different nature to the one obviously before us. What we see on the surface, therefore, these Zenosophists held, has significances which we can hardly discern, in another, co-existent order. Vrai knew this to be true of a kind, he told me thoughtfully, on the days when the light changed the slim limbs of his medlar tree into forms of soft silver, or when the dark waters in the carved cistern in his garden seemed to reflect back upon him depths far greater than the tank could in fact contain.

Yet Felix Vrai wondered if those Zenosophists knew more, unsaid. For surely if all things we know about in our world have an "other", or are also an "other", then it follows that the reverse must also be so: that this "other", who is also us, must be searching for us, seeking the glimpses that we also long for. We might be interlocking circles where only in an eye-shaped almondine zone where the two overlapped could any connection be made with what we truly are.

And this might explain for him the feeling that he sometimes had, and not he alone, he supposed, of being watched or followed or anyway not quite alone, even as he rested in his garden regarding the night. There was a Breton doctor, he said, Victor Segalen, a scholar of the Orient, who put it succinctly: "things half-seen can never be seen."

I can still recall the stillness of his studio room as silence fell after he had outlined to me the essence of the beliefs of these three sects that still eluded him. A lucent haze seemed to fall upon the air as the sun in the last of the dusk gave out its dying embers. The picture upon the chimney piece brooded in its brown light. I saw a glint upon the agate orb of an ornate cane in the oaken umbrella stand, like the spark of a struck flint. White rays emanated from the rose-water vessel. And in the grey eyes of Felix Vrai too there was a light I had not seen before.

I did not see my friend again. I noticed at first that we did not meet in chance encounters in the quarter where he lived, as had happened often enough before: nor, I found, had the humidor heard of him for a while. He had given me a key to his studio so that I might let myself in if ever he was late for our conversations. And so, with some deference (for I did not know if he was deep now in his studies and did not want to be disturbed), I entered the place to seek for him. He was not to be found, and nor (when I permitted myself to search his desk) was there any note indicating where he had gone. I looked desolately around the room for any clue about him. It was no longer as it had been when last we had met: it might have been empty for days; a frail fur of dust had settled upon it and the picture, the cane, the glass vessel, had all lost their remembered lustre.

I look for him still, or for his other, in the dim shadows of the streets of Istanbul, as it must now be called: and sometimes he seems to appear to me in the simulacra of faces and limbs seen in stones or trees. Perhaps somewhere, behind the veil, his bright form has found its home, eluding whatever lies in wait. But I think too how I stood that day at the top of the stone steps leading from the walled garden on the Bosphorus, above an empty mooring: and I looked out across the water to where the pale pennants of the sailing boats plied in the wan rays of the sun. One of those might, I hope now, have been his, at the start of a stranger voyage still, even than those he had found in the fallen capital and its empire of visions.

Carden in Capaea

Carden drew down the black blinds against the grey light of a rainy noon, and switched on the light-machine. While it wheezed into life, he caught up a richly woven cushion, with its scarlet swirls and golden interlacings, and struck it a few times. Dust escaped and became illuminated in the beam. He coughed and at once made a strange gesture with his left hand, not covering his mouth, but reaching out, then closing his fist.

"Capaean dust," he said, "caught in the market-place. Well now, what colour do you see?" he asked, pointing to the radiant motes.

There was a brief silence while we wondered what he meant. Then: "White"; "A sort of silver"; "Pale yellow", we variously offered. He nodded.

"Right. But aren't those the colours of the lantern's rays, rather than the dust? Now, watch if you will, this. Here, I am taught how to say the Capaean colours: and they try to teach me something else too, which I do not catch. This is Ezsenc."

On the screen, an old man, grinning through an ash-grey moustache, and wearing a white embroidered smock and vivid green pantaloons, held up his hand and spoke rapidly. The syllables were like nothing I had heard and I could see from my immediate companions' intent attitudes that they were unfamiliar to them as well, though we all had achievements in philology to our credit. Now, Ezsenc pointed to his shirt and slowly enunciated a word, which he followed with what must evidently be an explanation. Then he gestured to his trousers, gave out another word, and again there came more words afterwards.

There was a pause, and he waved his hands as if dismissing all that. Then he picked up from by his side a fat flask and held it up so that the sun, unseen, glinted in its glass, which was of a gamboge colour. He unstoppered it, then, holding it away, shook out carefully a few trickles of the water—or was it spirit?—within. Something precious, certainly. Staring now solemnly straight at the observer, he shrugged, and flickered his fingers, then angled his starkly shaped head. Knowing nothing of his old, and dying, language, I still felt his meaning, prompted by Carden's introduction, might be caught. He was saying, perhaps, "these (his clothes) have a colour: but what colour is this?"

The lantern blinked, and then transferred its gaze to a different scene. It came to rest on a censer in dimly seen chased silver, where it rested in a candle-lit stone niche. Fumes emanated slowly from it in graceful, trancing spirals. For a moment, as I sat on the hard chair in the bare hall, with its faint hint of disinfectant, it was as if the scent from this thurible had been transported to us, and the residue of cleaning fluid replaced with its rich, elusive essence of spices. The machine shifted itself again and an even older man, with a face of palimpsest, and wearing a long terracotta-hued garment, pointed first to his gown, and uttered a word, and then to the darkness that enfolded him, and then to the very faintly seen smoke. "He is Reflik, a sort of priest," Carden explained.

The priest uttered a short interrogatory word and his eyebrows, luxuriantly peppery, couched a question at us: then he lay his hand upon his chest and swayed gently forward slightly.

"What is he conveying there, Carden?" Latimer asked.

"I could not really tell. I thought at first it was: 'Upon my heart, I do not know what colour you would call these.' But later, I supposed it might be: 'I have the words within.' And since then I have imagined a third possibility: he is saying, perhaps, 'I am like that colour too, whatever it is.'"

Latimer adjusted his heavy spectacles. "Colour—or quality? Water and smoke—both, things one cannot grasp."

"Yes, that could be so," Carden conceded, "Yet it seemed to me that what they were trying to describe to me could be both a sort of colour, and a quality. There's just one more, and then I'll tell you how I came to encounter this. Excuse me . . . "

A further coughing fit possessed him, and he made again the quick stretching and seizing gesture. When he had recovered, he noticed us eyeing him. "I haven't got out of the habit yet," he explained. "That's how the Capaeans do it. The place is full of marsh fevers, and they're always spluttering. When they do, they reach out to steal back the breath they've shed."

"This is a Capaean boy, I did not take his name."

The youth, in white robes, watched with laughing approval by a coven of elders, took his turn in front of the camera. He had skin the complex, subtle, colour of ripe figs, with their same bloom too: and against this flesh there shone in mischief startlingly blue eyes, which were reflected in a bright blue kerchief, the only dash of colour against the brilliant light of his tunic. He pointed to this long piece of cloth, said a word, enjoying it upon his tongue: and then, squatting upon the ground, he plucked a stalk of bearded grass. He held this up, like a street conjurer, and then carefully inserted the fine nail of a forefinger into the stem, separating the green strands within. Looking up, he lifted high the finger and watched a bead of sap trickle down the taut flesh, before he quickly dipped his head, lapped up the moisture and returned his gaze ahead, a riddling twist to the corners of his mouth. The lantern's image faltered once more, and he was removed from us.

Carden, in gloom to one side of the projected light, seemed caught in thought for some moments. Then he recovered himself, switched off the machine and raised the lights in the hall. We took this as a signal to stir and shift in our chairs.

He stood before us, slight of figure, his sharp-featured face slightly softened by pale stubble, but still looking rather drawn.

"When I went to study the Capaeans," he resumed, "I was warned in Istanbul—warned that they would be hospitable, courteous, and compliant—but would smilingly tell me nothing. It did indeed take many months to learn anything from them. At first, they would not directly share any words of their language, but spoke to me only in the official tongue, as they do with all strangers and outsiders. They are a people—perhaps just four thousand of them now, and somewhat dispersed too—who have survived the centuries by what I would call a punctilious outward assimilation. One might say, they have never insisted upon themselves. Thus, it has been said, they have no history: they are a ghost people, glimpsed in the curt accounts of their overlords, of no consequence, willing homage-givers to whomever their patrons might happen to be—Persians, Tatars, Assassin lords, Ottomans, Russians. Three things, I think, have held them together still: their language, which they keep to themselves; certain subtle variations in the practice of whatever faith they have had to adopt; and a third thing, more difficult to distil, which I have tried to illustrate here; a knowledge of some kind."

He broke off to cough again, his hand barely keeping up with the fierce exhalations.

"As I say, they were reluctant to share any of these. But after a time, I started to pick up Capaean in a sly way. The men are very fond of a dice game, which I believe they would play all day if they could, in the cafés and taverns. By watching them from a nearby table in the hushed cool of the late evening, I began to see what the rules might be and I asked, much to their astonishment, if I might join in. They play for small stakes, you know, and the chance to rook an intruder vied in them with what I must call a certain natural gallantry that made them reluctant to have too vast an advantage over me. So they compromised with their consciences, and took time to explain the rules more. And it turned out, of course, that since this was a Capaean game, all its throws and scores and other special terms of art were in their own tongue. And that was how I first insinuated myself into the mystery of their near-lost language.

"Well, I can tell you, as I'm sure some of you discerned," (here he was being indulgent, since none of us had his specialist understanding of the vocabularies in the Black Sea region), "that it has some distant affinity with Georgian, but it is not, not by any means, as the Tbilisi scholars would claim, merely an archaic dialect of that. And one of the special things about it, one of the things I liked, is this idea they have of—of, well, let me explain it this way. They have a word in the dice game for the throw that comes from nowhere, the least expected cast, one that shifts the run of the game decisively away from where it was. I thought at first this word was just the equivalent of our "chance", or even that coy phrase "lady luck". But it is not so: to them, this sort of turn in fortune is more like a breath upon the dice, a gust of the unseen. When it happened, the usual amicable chatter and banter would halt: then one of them would say it, softly, though it seemed to me semi-reluctantly. The first time I barely heard it and they passed on: but when it happened again, I persisted, and pretended to get annoyed that they were hiding some secret rule or trick from me: and so then, they did try to explain it, and saw that I was lost, and we proceeded by analogy, and so led on to talk of the things that have colour, the things of this world, and the things that have no colour that can be known."

Carden then said more about the culture of the Capaeans, and demonstrated to us phrases in their language. He asked, what we all ask ourselves, what was the point of his work: why try to learn and preserve just one among the hundreds of dying tongues in the world? Then he became quite lyrical.

"The language we have surely sets limits to what we perceive, doesn't it? I have known races that had terms for the finest gradations of things that to the West are all alike: it is a wonder to listen, for example, to the Marmorean fisherman talk on sea-currents, or to the Red Delta people on the flights and migrations of water-birds, or the Almarack goatherds on the ways of the winds upon their mountains. Every single lost word, I sometimes think, is a lost chance of understanding the world that others can see."

As people made their departures, the plump, roseate Wharton, who never ventures beyond the regions of the Romance languages ("go wherever they have fourteen words for siesta and twenty-two for how to drink wine, my boy," he once boomed at me), came up to Carden, solicitously.

"I like all that talk of a colour which is not, Carden. Very intriguing. No such stuff among the Latins, you know. Though it reminds me of certain terms in Zarphatic—things the Provençal Jews tried to convey, that they had seen in Carcassone or Arles. But—here now, your own colour, Carden, is positively grim. Go and see the lab boys in Tropicals, do—you've picked up more than Caspian dust, I think."

It was typical of him to mis-remember, so soon, where Carden had been: but I thought his advice was good, and I certainly shared his concern.

Carden had signalled to me during the concluding chatter at the end of the lecture, and I lingered until I was the last left. We had known each other for what seemed many years. I can't say exactly what first drew us toward one another. We both worked on the edges of things—I in the Baltic and the peri-Arctic, he in the Bosphorus and the Black Sea littorals. And in languages that formed no part of the great tree from which most others grew. But I don't suppose that was all. Sometimes there is just an affinity, and that is all that can be said.

"There's something more I wanted to share with you," he explained, smiling, and I strode beside his lean form through the hesitant rain towards his quarters. Above us, the clouds were a mingling of smeared grey and stained white, like tapestries of wet ash, all but for one chance burst of blue they had not yet covered. Since Carden was seldom in England, he did not need much to live in here, and had what was called a garden room at the back of a somewhat distressed late-Georgian house in a decaying square. That one room, with paned doors looking out onto a narrow walled wilderness, served as his study, library, living-room and bedroom, for a great leather couch occupied its centre, positioned so that it faced the doors, to the wild retreat beyond. A shelf and a chest held carved boxes, bronze candlesticks, a serrated dagger, and a grinning mask, gifts from the peoples he'd visited.

He dropped into the piled cushions on his couch, releasing much dust, and coughed repeatedly, all the while gesturing as he had said the Capaeans do: a swift opening of the fingers, then a quick gripping. Recovering a little, he motioned me to a threadbare red armchair.

"I want you to know. Wharton's warning is too late. It was well-meant, but they've already looked at me, and don't know what they can do. Whatever it is, it is new to them. Not a disease they know: not one they've trapped and labelled. So I'm simply waiting."

I stared at him, mute. I was taken aback by his fatalism, not sure just what he meant when he said he was only waiting.

I whispered and gestured to him to rest and be quiet, but he shook his head.

"There's more I want to say. When I had been there a few weeks and had gone out to their farthest villages to find the words that might be the oldest of all, I did get taken by their marsh fevers. You see, of course, they occupy marginal land: whatever nobody else wants. There's just tough husks of juiceless grass—useless for anything—and stagnant pools of black water, and a few crabby trees, for miles. Here I wandered too long, I admit. I had it bad for five days or more, I'm not sure, and, as you see, I haven't thrown it off yet. They brought me to one of their reed-thatched wooden huts, and the boy Drustann—you saw him on the film—came to tend to me, overseen by the women and sometimes an elder. My sight was very wobbly. I would see them approach, vaguely, in blurred silhouette, with a drink, or broth, or to wave fumigations over me, and I would accept gratefully, and then I would not see them go. They would just dissolve back into the dimness—or somehow into me, I was not sure which. Imagine someone bending over your bed, their shadow cast by the constant lamp suddenly darkening your eyes, and then the feeling that this shadow of theirs was exactly matching itself to your own form.

"When I could at last get up and walk, with the boy's help, I was still terribly weakened. And light-headed. Funny phrase, isn't it? But it's right. I felt as if all the rest of my body was barely there. And freed from that burden, I had the sense I could, if I tried, move simply by dissolving myself, as if I were just a force or an impulse and nothing more. I rested on a fallen tree trunk and put my sight to the horizon and felt this sudden lunge as if I could, if I wanted, just go where my gaze went."

"All the effect of the fever, of course," I put in.

There was a silence, broken only by the beat of the rain, which had become more rapid.

"You know the most curious thing about the Capaeans?" he continued. "It isn't by any means unique to them, that I know. Old fat Wharton was right about the Zarphatics, and I dare say you've seen it in Lithuania or Karelia too. It's the way they've survived by somehow not being there—do you know what I mean? No matter what conqueror swept over them, no matter what faith, or—or fealty—they were required to adopt—they would later be found again, still with what was theirs. It is as if they had the ability to fade away when the enemy came. I don't mean like partisans, carrying on the struggle in the hills or whatever. I mean, they had the ability to disappear, though they were also all the while under their assailant's rule.

"You saw that they introduced me to some idea they had about dust, water, smoke, sap. And they seemed to ask in each case: 'What is it?' Well, do you know what was the most frustrating thing of all? Sometimes they made as if to show me other things of the same kind, and ask the same question: 'What is it?' Drustann, for example, did it all the time. But I couldn't see what they, or he, meant. And I didn't know if they were jesting or in earnest. But it made me wonder if they might be a people who have the same perception of the elusive as those others, those who see far more of the seas, the birds or the winds. I have to get back there to find out more, you know. This other thing, whatever it is, keeps calling me. Sometimes at night I dream I am there. I *shall* go back."

The room had darkened and there was a white sweat glinting upon his forehead and cheeks. I handed him a bright blue piece of rag from where it had dropped by his side, and he held it to his flesh.

I was put in mind of a question, which I aimed at him as lightly as I could. "So the young man was called Drustann, was he? You couldn't name him when you showed the film. He must have been very devoted."

"Yes. Yes, his name, er, eluded me for a moment then."
Or, I thought, he did not want to give it then. What isn't
named, isn't known—was that what he had said?

He sank back and resumed coughing and making his catching
gesture—catching, but not, I noticed, clutching this time,
as he had before. I asked him what I could do, but he just
stared at me as if from another's eyes.

A short while after, so as not to tire him further, I left.
His prematurely paled hair lay flat upon his sharply-whetted
skull, and his eyes were deep and dark in their sockets. I stood
upon the doorstep, looking back into his room, at the worn
books, bare furniture, unlit fireplace, wooden shelf with its
ancient strange things from the far lands he'd seen, and at
the brief bright blaze of blue that lay beside him. Then I
went out into the wild garden, with its damp dank slabs of
stone, dressed in bright moss, and its blue wicket gate beaded
with rain drops. I was trying to remember all I could of our
conversation, especially exactly what he'd said about how
we limit what we discern by the things we can name. And I
gazed back again at his glazed garden doors, as if this might
help me remember. But, what with the quickening rain, and
the gathering dusk, there was nothing to be known beyond,
except flickering shadow and uncertain shapes: or, nothing
I could name.

The Bookshop in Nový Svět

As Assistant Actuary Hrobar clopped down the staircase, his waistcoat chain bouncing, his brown derby hat wobbling precariously on his head, and his teeth grimly clenching his unlit pipe, he met, slowly easing himself up to his attic room, the artist Capcek. They kept almost exactly opposite hours. The clerk was at his office punctually from nine a.m. until four p.m. The illustrator preferred to work in twilight and at night. His main commissions, Hrobar knew, were for funeral stationery, memorial cards and commemorative brochures, for which he made tasteful designs, with dignified flourishes and discreet emblems, in the only two colours he was allowed, sable and violet. When he had first moved in to the narrow, sloping cell, with its one good window overlooking the square, Capcek had invited Hrobar up and showed him some of his work. It looked good to the Assistant Actuary, discreet, deft, but—though he knew much about the ways of death—he knew he was no judge of art (after all, he was from Brno), so he had merely murmured polite praise. They hailed each other as they passed, the artist very slender, with short sawdust-coloured hair and eyes the shiny brown of horse chestnuts when, in autumn, they ease out from their spiked green shells.

Hrobar paused at the outer entranceway, clamped a wad of Old Devil mixture into the encrusted bowl of his pipe, struck a match, and held it as he drew with unction upon the stem. Blue fumes scented his flesh. Then he set off, passing the great ornate lampposts and the good tall stone buildings, with their iron balconies and finials, at a steady pace as he did each working morning, noting the wisps of white mist still lingering among the increasingly leafless trees, and sending plumes of tobacco smoke to join them. At his destination, he took the five steps to the great glazed doors with his customary care, extracted the pipe and held the warm bowl in the palm of his hand, and made his way to the little office where he had worked for twenty-four years.

Tomas Hrobar kept the Tables of Mortality for the Workmen's Compensation Society. These were no simple matter, and required a methodical brain but not an unquestioning one. Some years ago, an official, presumed to be much more learned than he, had established that three factors affected the prosperity and security of the Society, that is to say, the exact balance between what it paid out and what it took in. Those factors were: the type of trade or industry pursued by a workman; where he lived; and what part, if any, he had played in the late war. Provided with information on these matters, all in his neat columns, Assistant Actuary Hrobar could work out at what point any workman might be expected to cease being able to work, or to leave his wife and orphans altogether to the care of the Society. This in turn suggested—though that was not a matter for him—the amount of weekly subscription the individual should pay from his wages. However, it was not only such averages that Hrobar calculated, for he must also remain alert to strange clusters, where the general rules of the Tables of Mortality appeared to be usurped by some wrinkle in the sable roll of fatality, which must be smoothed out by his expert hands. And everyone in the Society agreed that Hrobar was very good at what he did, that he had an instinctive flair for it.

There could also be extra complications, and yet these did not daunt him. He remembered how once a certain

Doctor K, a weary but kindly young man, with ears pointed back like a bat and sleek dark hair, had persuaded him that improvements he had instigated in the working conditions of a certain group of subscribers, would henceforth raise their expectancies, and therefore lower their subscriptions. Hrobar had never heard of any official of the Society advocating this approach before, but he followed the logic and would have made the necessary adjustments to his Tables. But his boss, Herr Salus, had been shaking his head sceptically behind the limpid-eyed young man, and, when he had gone, he told Hrobar not to bother. "Those improvements he has suggested will never be made," he said, simply.

Unusually, silver-haired Salus was waiting for him by his desk, picking his fingernails with a letter-opener. The Assistant Actuary greeted him heartily, but with perhaps a slightly wary tinge to his tone, for he did not like his day to be disturbed, but preferred rather to get straight on with the Tables. Salus asked him if he had enjoyed a good evening. Hrobar fingered his watch-chain and tried to remember what he had done, as if much depended upon his answer. He had read the *Gazette*, he remembered that, and he had eaten a red stew at some point, and he had looked out of the window quite a lot. None of those seemed worth reporting. So he said merely that he had, it had been restful.

Herr Salus beckoned him towards his own, bigger and rather better-appointed office.

"I am very pleased to tell you, Hrobar, that I am being promoted, out of the Actuary's Department, towards the Expansion Department. I will be in charge of offering our help to even more workmen. It is a great honour." The thin pink lips made a slit like a smile. Hrobar listened intently. Was he to be told, then, that he would now move into his boss's place? An elevation for him, too? He drew back in his chair and tightened his paunch.

"There is another matter, I Hrobar, which affects you personally."

"Yes, Herr Salus?"

"Yes. You see, we shall not be needing you any further. The Actuary's Department is, to be frank, to be completely closed down."

It was characteristic of Hrobar that his first thought was not for himself, but for the Society. Who would maintain the Tables of Mortality now? Who would know how to balance out the brevity and longevity of so many lives? Very slowly and carefully, he put these questions. The hand of Herr Salus raised a long white pointed finger.

"It is all being simplified, Hrobar, old man. Some bright spark at the top has worked it all out. It is very ingenious. Everyone will pay the same flat rate."

The almost-former actuary struggled to comprehend this. "But the risk . . . "

"There will be no risk. The flat rate will naturally be set at what it was for the higher end of the mortality spectrum. Many will pay more, but it will be much simpler for them. Now, as to your own concerns, Mr. Hrobar—the Society is not at all unappreciative of your good and long service, and . . . "

The remaining words passed the clerk by in a blur. "Parting payment, enough for a few months certainly . . . and a modest stipend . . . sound references, of course, model employee, a good head, industrious . . . "

Hrobar went back to his office, filed all the Tables carefully (he was sure they would be needed again), strolled around the echoing corridors of the building to let a few acquaintances know, affecting unconcern to them, and then placed in a waxed paper bag the minor personal items he had here: a calendar, some certificates, a pencil sharpener made from part of a brass shell. As he made to leave the grand old edifice for the last time, Hrobar could not stop himself from blurting out to Herr Salus: "But what am I to do now?"

73

"Do now?" The thin shoulders shrugged and the little dank slot once more appeared in the lips. "Do? Why, *ah*—enjoy life, you know! You've got a bit put by, I don't doubt, and with this subvention from the Society, why, err—" He looked at Hrobar doubtfully. "Try music, the theatre, why not poetry?" Then his jaw let out a ratchety laugh, and he waved him away, part cheerily, part in dismissal.

Tomas Hrobar took a long route home. Crossing the Great Bridge, he stopped to watch a puppet vendor joggling his stringed wooden dolls in the hope of catching the attention of children or whimsical visitors. The painted faces spun round as if missing nothing, and the limbs jerked spasmodically. The puppet-seller's long black coat was worn, and his face was the dry faded white of old newspaper.

Reaching the other side, the old clerk soon took a seat outside a café on the river bank and ordered himself a cinnamon schnitzel and a coffee with warm milk. He sat in the muted sunlight under the dappling of the sycamore trees and his mind for a few moments became mostly contentless, or at least pursued no fixed object of thought, but rather drifted slowly and opaquely on, like the brown waters below. Then he asked for an apricot brandy and sipped it with simple ceremony. Finally, he set the Old Devil going again in his pipe and watched the lavender blue fumes drift out across the river. Well, what had that brittle bodied sceptic Salus thrown at him, eh? Poetry! We shall see, he said to himself, we shall see about that.

Capcek was applying some violet ink to an angel's trumpet when Hrobar called upon him, having heaved his form up the four flights of stairs in the dwindling light. As soon as he heard his neighbour's news, he set down his pen and poured him a black spirit he kept in a stone flask, then thoughtfully looked inside a dried-up ink well, shook it a little, and added some of the spirit to it for himself. He ran his fingers through the short blond sawdust hair. They inhaled the spirit quietly for a while. Then the attic dweller walked to his one window, let at a curious angle into the sloping roof, and distinctly trapezoidal in shape, and gazed out. From here, without looking at him, he addressed the ex-actuary assistant.

"Hrobar," he said, "Don't take this amiss. A man of your record, your brains . . . no trouble . . . certain to get a place. But, if not, quite possible, well, with my contacts, can get you perhaps a bit, sometimes, a 'professional mourner' you see? Nothing to it, except looking solemn and walking slowly."

Hrobar felt touched by his acquaintance's generous concern.

"I'm all right for a while," he said. "But tell me, Capcek, as an artist, you know, do you happen to have any poetry?"

The younger man's fair eyebrows twitched as if they were inquisitive caterpillars. "Poetry, Hrobar? Well, yes, I have some. Any particular sort?"

His visitor shrugged.

"No. I would just like to borrow some to have a look at it."

The murmur of the square came gently up to the quarter-opened sash window of Tomas Hrobar's room. It was impossible, really, to distinguish anything individual from it; along with the birds and trees, the wind, the fountain, there were voices certainly, each saying something the speaker thought worth mentioning on this dying early autumn day, but all lost in that constant undertone, the city's tongue of dust and soot.

The resident heard this without hearing it, as always, and it lulled him somehow as he turned the brittle white pages of a volume called *Scarlet Orchids*. The words, he observed, were not like those he read in the *Gazette*, and the thread of them was difficult to follow. There were faint rivulets of black type which, taken together, would hardly fill a single report in the newspaper, a court report, say, or the account of a hot air balloon rally, or a speech on production in the North Bohemian coalfields. As far as Hrobar could make out, though, the author thought that the scarlet orchids of his title might one day take it upon themselves to put on a black top hat, and a tailcoat, place their green stems in well-buffed shoes, and stalk the quarters of the city looking for sins equal to those they dreamed of when they were in the hothouse or the vase. Indeed, the poet (one Arturo Vassi) implied that they might already be up to this trick, and some of those people we might pass and greet in the streets of dusk could very well be orchids in disguise. Despite himself, Hrobar went to look out of the window onto the square.

Later, he politely returned the volume to Capcek, and said—very much to the artist's surprise—that he must not keep it, but he would like to find one for himself.

"Try the Jackdaw Bookshop, in Nový Svět, halfway down—narrow door, old green paint, easy to miss," his friend advised.

Before returning to the black plumes of the memorial card design he was working on, he watched Hrobar's broad retreating back, with a gentle wonderment, and shook his head.

The inside of the Jackdaw Bookshop, when it eventually opened, reminded Hrobar of what it might be like to be suspended in a glass of Capcek's black spirit. The atmosphere was thick and dark, and yet there was a decided sharp tang about it, caused in part by the haughty demeanour of the angular-faced, long-locked proprietor. He laughed when, after searching the sloping shelves in vain, Hrobar asked after a copy of *Scarlet Orchids*.

"You won't get that anywhere."

"Why is that ?"

A disdainful drawing in of the nostrils.

"Hadn't you heard? Vassi died three days ago."

"I see. He had been ill?

"No. Weary."

"Ah. And, after, his family withdrew all his books?"

"*Tscha*, don't they wish they could. No, no. There was a run on his books, of course. Collectors. You could get twice the price for them now, more."

Hrobar considered this information judiciously.

"Does that always happen? When poets die?"

A sigh. "Of course not. Only when young poets die. Old Alfred Kablin passed away at eighty-two last week and no-one rushed after his stuff, I can tell you. If you'd like eight copies of *Sobieski at the Gates*, all four hundred pages of very blank verse, I can oblige. What? What have I got that is *like Scarlet Orchids*? My dear man . . . "

Tomas Hrobar came away from the shop with one copy only of Kablin's marmoreal master-work, and a very narrow, very thin volume, *The Purple Serpent*. He took a seat in the park, lit his pipe, and studied these intently. In the newer volume, the text was not in straight columns, but in sinuous curves across the two open pages, over and on to the next two, and so on. It told of how a great kraken had taken hold of the city and was leaving in its wake a spoor of dusk and melancholy. The courtyards and cobbled slopes, it said, the gardens and little hidden squares, were all, if you looked carefully, infiltrated by its sombre breath or its subtle crystal slime. For all its air of pondered gloom, though, Hrobar thought there was something sportive about the way the words curved over the white sheets, and he said to himself that he did not see this poet dying of weariness soon.

After dipping into Kablin's tome, though, he thought that he himself might emulate Arturo Vassi if he read much longer. So he put the book aside, and considered. It ought to be possible, he thought, to work out a triangulation for poets, just as his former employer had for workmen, before they foolishly abandoned the beautiful precision in fatality-forecasting that he himself had practised so well and so long. And then, to buy up just the right volumes, at the right time, ready to sell them again at a significant margin when the versifier died. But what would be the factors in triangulating poets? Could they be the same as for workmen? To take their trade, first. Would the cheery ditties of the Whistling Postman of Wenceslasville (he had observed his many pamphlets scattered on the newspaper stand where he bought his Gazette) suggest a lower level of risk than, say, the volume called *Zrak! Zrak!*, by a furious futurist, which the assistant at the Jackdaw had suspended like a pale concertina from his roof-beam? And, as for place, might a rural schoolmaster with his *Almond-Blossoms*, be reasonably expected to linger a good deal longer than a cabaret-lounger and bar-fly here in the capital? Certainly. And as to the war, well, he was not sure if that was a special consideration with poets. If it wasn't, by all the laws he had learned, there must be some other third thing he must discover and then, using a new version of the Tables he had compiled, he might soon be on to something.

"You again?" Hrobar had made his way back to the Jackdaw Bookshop. The same flavour of dark asperity hung in the air. "Well? I'm not taking back that Kablin, if that's what you want."

"No. It's about *The Purple Serpent*."

"What about it?"

"It doesn't have an author."

"Yes it does. It says, 'By Z.' "

"I see that. But who is Z?"

"He who has been the Serpent."

Hrobar looked at him shrewdly.

"You."

A flick of black locks and a sly smile.

"My dear sir, I have never been known to recommend any book except my own. What did you think of it?"

"It is not at all like *Scarlet Orchids*."

"Oh, you say? Yet we are seen as of the same school. And Vassi was a visionary, you know. I have half a mind to follow after him."

"You won't."

A narrowing of the bookseller's black eyes.

"You seem very sure of that."

"I liked your book. I'm nothing literary, but I have a theory. Also, in its way, a business proposition. You see . . . "

The author and bookseller called Z. had not scorned the outline that the revived actuary had put to him. We are not being macabre, Hrobar had argued. Poets will die, and when they die young, usually, their work will suddenly sell well. It has happened, you tell me, so often as to be a rule in your trade. Very well, then we must find a way of predicting which poets are going to succumb, and discreetly acquire all we can of their rarest works. I do the predicting, you do the acquiring and selling. I will go in with you on that, so that the investment—and the proceeds—are shared. Further, it is no good going after the poets who are obviously ill, as everyone will see what is to happen with them: we must discern those that are to all appearances sound, yet have already heard on the wind the tolling of the green bell that calls us to the grave. Quite poetic itself, said Z, smirking. You're on. They shook hands. Tomas Hrobar went away with a pile of loaned poetry books to study.

In a long life devoted to figures and the remorseless working-out of a dry logic, Hrobar had never given much thought or time to the arts. But as he walked home, he found himself peering watchfully at well-dressed gentlemen in their shining evening wear, in case they should happen to be merely the sheath for—ludicrous thought—a walking orchid. And he caught himself looking too into the sequestered courtyards and dead-end byways, to see if there might be some tinted ichor lurking there, masking the walls with sadness. He knew these fancies were foolish—yet somehow they stayed with him. How was it possible that poets, and perhaps storywriters too, could breathe such figures into the streets? How many others, like him, read them and then acted as if they were real—until, until they almost became real?

Capcek called down to see him that evening. Tentatively, delicately, he advanced his suggestion—how were his funds? A funeral tomorrow, if he would welcome a small honorarium. The family forbidden, or refusing, or both. A few friends and associates, also some professional mourners, including himself. Very simple. Precede the cortège at a stately pace from the house to the cemetery. Hrobar nodded, more to oblige his friend. Soon, he expected to have a reasonable supply of funds, but until then . . .

Dull grey slabs of cloud lay across the city as Capcek and Hromar walked ahead of the slow-stepping horses, through a labyrinth of streets where the walls seemed to want to clutch at each other, lurching forwards towards a stone embrace they never achieved. There was scarcely room even for the mean, black-draped cart to pass. Children with glinting eyes and shawled women with pale faces watched as they negotiated the steep, dim roads to the graveyard on the hill. The horses shied and whinnied often, and once when, forgetting decorum, Hrobar turned to quieten them, they reared away and almost upset the burden behind. He quickly resumed his role. The priest read through the burial service in haste. A few hands reached forward to throw white orchids—scarlet ones were not to be had—upon the coffin lid, even as the first scatterings of soil descended. The undertaker signalled Capcek and Hromar away, as their task was done, but they were stopped at the lych-gate by a cluster of mourners who had gathered there, the literary friends of the deceased. A tall man in a quaint frock-coat, bronze-green at its edges, invited them to join the wake. They looked at the director, who shrugged. Behind Hromar's ear, the bookseller from the Jackdaw murmured, "I had no idea you would be here. Say yes, it's a great opportunity to measure some of them up." But both Hrobar and Capcek politely declined.

The actuary took the bookseller by the arm as the party turned away.

"I do not need to meet them, I tell you. I never met any of the workmen whose fates I calculated. Yet I was very often right, you see. It is all in the tables of mortality, that is all."

For some weeks afterwards, the clerk shut himself up in his room and sifted the facts about all the poets in the city and the country that he could lay his hands on, often returning from the Jackdaw with great armfuls of books to read and consult. At the end of this prolonged period of fact-taking and calculating, he began to construct his Tables. He had decided that, as with workmen, the factors of trade or industry—and even locality—remained constant, and must still be used. But he did not see that the war entered into matters so much for poets, despite the gallantry that some had undoubtedly displayed, and so he searched for the elusive third factor, which he was convinced was to be found, in some form, in the works of the poets. For the time being, he labelled it "I", for Imagination, and he assessed from what he read the tendency of the poet's thought and dreamings, and added these to the other two sides of the triangle. Yet he was not very satisfied by that: it would have to do, until he more precisely defined it. The casting of the Tables complete, he sat and brooded upon the calculations for a few days more. Where was there a flaw? He could discover none.

At the end of his studies, he took the result to the author called Z, at the Jackdaw, who thrust back his long black hair and scowled.

"Jakub Iblis? Jakub Iblis? *The Lantern Garden*? I hardly think so. Tepid, timorous, looks a mere sliver, I give you that, but plenty of money, lives in the High Quarter, and never seems to stir an eyelid at anything. Still, if you say so . . . "

Hrobar looked out from Capcek's trapezoidal window that evening. The poet Iblis was right, he thought. Viewed from an eyrie such as this, the great lamps on their iron stems were like huge white and amber blooms, and all the city a vast park of their illuminated flowers. And suppose, as the poet suggested, those golden and silver blossoms one day began to fade and decay, to turn brown, like a gutted wick? "*When the lamplight flickers, the shadows dance.*"

The artist had been watching him at intervals, as he worked on limning a weeping fig in one margin of a memorial brochure.

"Do you remember that mean neighbourhood we had to go to for poor Vassi's funeral?" he asked. "I had never strayed there before. All those huddled hovels. Well, here's a thing, in the *Gazette*. Some poor woman—you remember the wretches we saw?—frightened almost out of her wits by a stranger who followed her in those same streets, up into the great houses beyond. No, he didn't touch her. He just loomed out of the murk behind her all the while, and filled her with dread. A great black shadow, she said, strangely shaped, and a cloak playing and billowing about him all the time, and seeming to twist itself into numbers, as it might be a great fat eight or a pointing seven. She has put the fear of it into all the washerwomen and seamstresses of those streets, so they won't go on errands up there anymore. And that's really why the paper reports it, you see: very jokey, a strike of the slatterns, on a flimsy pretext."

His friend nodded thoughtfully.

"Have you any more of that black spirit? I don't mind drinking from the inkwell this time."

"So," said the author of *The Purple Serpent*, "you were right. I don't know how, but you were. Iblis is gone, and all those opuscules of his I carefully garnered at your behest have tripled in value. We've done very well. Who's next? I hope it isn't someone I know—too well."

Tomas Hrobar sat down heavily on a wooden chair, and his watch-chain settled itself into place.

"What did you do exactly, when you wrote your book?"

"How do you mean? You're not saying I'm next? You assured me before . . . "

"No, of course not. I was just curious. What was it like, to write such a strange thing?"

The proprietor of the Jackdaw stroked his sleek black hair, which looked for the moment rather like the plumage of the bookshop's patron bird, limned on the woodcut he used for its emblem.

"What was it like? It was like writing the truth, my friend. Like saying just exactly what must be said, no more. I told you I was he who sees the Serpent, and that wasn't a joke. I saw it uncoil in my head, and I sent it down into the streets . . . "

"Where it yet has its lair and still leaves its spoor."

"Really, old Tomas, you are indeed getting poetic. You think the snake writhes still? If only my writing were that potent."

"Listen. I may only be an old actuary. But after I had carefully compiled my Tables for predicting the death of poets, I found there was something left, unaccounted for. And so, I entered a formula. I called it 'I' for Imagination. I meant the hidden hints in their verse, you see, which I thought I could assess, and, and—add to the triangulation. This was wrong. I was straying from the iron path of objective fact. That 'I' was truly I, was *my* imagination, not theirs. I am no poet, but I have brooded like you, and I have also sent something down into the streets in my form, in the shapes that I see: a phantom made of numbers. How do I get it back?"

The bookseller looked at him with something like pity in his hatchet face. "Come, out into the light a little." They stood on the mossed cobbles in the high-walled street which wound its sinuous way down to the great river. "You can't. This isn't a city that ever lets its images go. And I'll tell you one thing more. Don't reproach yourself too much. For I'm not so sure whether we dream the city, or the city dreams us."

The Autumn Keeper

Simon Marmoresh collected prodigies: he had them come to him in the hothouse made for him high on the flat roof of the old water tower on Petrin Hill. Here, on the least regarded summit above the city, he could lean on the parapet and train his jaded gaze upon the jagged silhouettes of Castle Hill and the dark mass of Cemetery Hill, and then on all of the towers, spires and angular stone canopies below. And, seen by strangers pausing in the courtyards or the twisting streets and passages of the city, his mansard domain would sometimes send quick glinting signals of crystalline light, as if it were some way-station conveying messages from the hidden stars.

The green-tinged glass of his humid retreat threw an olive hue upon the faces and the flesh of his guests, and accentuated the contours of his own countenance, which was skeletal and ascetic, the skin like the frail tissue that guards engravings in old books. Very fine green veins ran beneath, like the rivers in a lost country on a faded map. His hair was a coating of hoar-frost, sharp and white.

As they paced the close space of his glass studio, all among the lolling exotic blooms, the invited virtuosi, the wastrels, wanderers and idealists he had summoned from the streets below, sometimes seemed to him interchangeable with his beloved, languid-leaved plants, his streaked orchids, palpitant white lilies, star-flowers, or the ancient, gnarled-barked cycads.

One evening in October, some of his visitors, the fine silver ichor of their cigarettes vying with the sensual fumes of the flowers, amused themselves by guessing what peculiar accomplishments had attracted Marmoresh to his latest mortal finds. There might be a modernist at the cimbalom, perhaps, or the most skilled sardonyx-carver in the Double Monarchy, the discoverer of an ancient Assyrian incense, all replete with the sap of the cedar and the juice of the cypress, or maybe a mask-maker, sky-watcher, ikon-faker, toy-repairer, soul-barer, or even (it could be) simply an old veteran whose slow grave grace at petanque their host might have observed in the park on his hill, passing by one dusk, under a sunset of polished copper.

In particular, they regarded a young man who was standing uncertainly near the paned door, trying to look nonchalant. He was not handsome, but he was so near to it that he attracted more stares even than a conventional comeliness might earn. He had wide, violet eyes, a mere faint smudge of eyebrows, a delicate nose, just slightly tilted cheekbones, and a soft mouth of rhubarb-pink. He wore his dark hair short, and fiercely brushed in firm bristles. All in all, it was a very curious composition.

"Well, what of him?" asked the apothecary Hardouin, with a sly nod. But silence fell on this occasion, and the little coterie found it could not even venture a surmise about the boy. At length, one of them, Julian, a florist who tortured his severed flowers into the strangest of shapes, took pity upon his awkwardness and approached him with a solicitude that he almost fooled himself was kindness.

"Have you been the rounds?" he asked, "Tonight the master has gathered for us a bunch of soothsayers, you know. He has plucked them from below. You must have your destiny told. It would be a waste not to. Besides, even if you don't want to hear it, if I am frank, *we* all do. We do." And he gestured with a wide arc of his arm at the staring set he had just left, brushing against a giant frog-fern that squatted in a bulbous pot in the corner. "Now, let's see . . . " And he guided the youth, with a gentle pressure, towards one of the street-prophets Marmoresh had assembled.

The tower-owner had been out upon one of his nocturnal wanderings in the Far Quarter, looking for all the most picturesque, secret, vagrant or evidently bogus fortune-tellers, and his ready purse had soon fetched them up the steep iron stairs of his retreat.

This edifice, though made in dim red brick, had been modelled, at the whim of some forgotten municipal architect, upon a Flemish bell-tower, a slender column with a wider platform at its peak, all garnished with blind mock-arches, castellations like wolf's teeth, and a few strange niches which seemed to need votive figurines. When, after a few decades, it had proved to be not quite up to its mechanic task, Marmoresh had purchased it, and had it converted for use as his home and eyrie. Here, he had exercised too, an eye for irony: for his own fortune had been acquired from a mineral water.

As a young man, he had formed a simple economic theory, that the way to riches was to take a profuse and inexpensive commodity and paint it for the aspiring bourgeoisie as in reality a rare and luxurious thing. Pursuing this, and aided principally by his charm and ardour, he had taken a share in the business of a modest Swabian table-water, poured the liquid into a new cobalt-blue Cubist bottle, all sharp facets, with a stark label, and baptised it CASTALIA.

Soon, suitably induced, all the haughtiest waiters of the smartest restaurants and hotels of Basel and Nice, Klagenfurt and Ascona, were recommending it to their patrons in conspiratorial tones, affecting it to be a very rare elixir: and those who had shunned it before in its old, tubby, plain bottle, now clamoured for the blue flask and its crystal contents.

Marmoresh, the master of this legendary fount in a secluded, sighing little spa town, with its trim pines and lavender fields, perpetuated the myth of its scarcity by a cool control of supply, amply proving the practicality of his theory and pocketing the proceeds of his inspiration. Now, he had long relinquished the day to day affairs of the business to others, but affection for the trade had been in part why he had bought the old water tower upon Petrin Hill, where it stood in its own compound, at the opposite end of the summit from the panorama, the hall of mirrors and the ornamental gardens.

In the green twilight, lit only be a paring of moon and a few pale oil-lamps, his guests drifted like viridian spirits, speaking, as if the hushed light had diminished their voices too, mostly in whispers. Marmoresh himself glided amongst them in his neat, dark city garb, listening and watching, and occasionally feeding titbits of over-ripe fruit to his constant companion, Timoleon, a ring-tailed lemur. With his dark eye-markings like ancient spectacles, his little fringe of fur at the jaw, and his small crooked paws, the creature might pass in the dim light as one of his human acquisitions, a scribbler from some narrow attic perhaps, or a fusty bookseller, or professor of an arcane study. The lemur regarded each of the company gravely as it nibbled pensively upon a slice of medlar, and some shifted uneasily under his stare. The pet was of course rumoured really to be the mineral-water master's familiar and wisest counsellor, and the murmured conversations Marmoresh held with him, a mingling of human speech, and a series of tongue-clickings and gibberings, did not dispel the idea.

Solemnly, the lemur's master presided as each of his prophets plied his trade, whether with the proffered palms of the guests, or by scrying in an opaque crystal globe, by studying painted cards, or simply by staring hard at the face before them. And, as Julian approached, adjusting his boutonnier made of a chrysanthemum of tarnished gold, and guiding the boy towards the cenacle of seers, the eyes of their host seemed to take upon themselves an especially keen gleam.

"Armand," he said, "I am glad you came. Here, why don't you try my—amusements?"

He had found the boy as he prowled one day in the dwindling light: he was sketching a street lantern. There were artists enough in the city for sure, but something about his fierce preoccupation with the task had drawn Marmoresh closer. Gently, he had won his confidence a little, and found that the young man drew nothing else; his whole oblong portfolio, in tattered paper wrappers, was a lamp album, holding hundreds of pictures in pencil or wan ink of the dark columns, and the elegant rhomboids, globes and candelabra of the city lights. This Armand had a normal boy's passion for collecting, listing and cataloguing, but in him this had taken a peculiar flight of fancy, for he gave each light a title and summoned it by a few words which implied for each an entire tale. He could get very little out of the young artist about his past, other than that he had grown up in a remote Moravian village with a mother who was half-French; both parents, Marmoresh inferred, had perished in the late war. He gave the boy his card and told him about the soirées he held in his hothouse studio. Clinging to his book of drawings and fidgeting a little, this Armand had listened patiently enough, but Marmoresh had not been persuaded he would respond.

Before he turned to resume his restless wandering—

"What will you do when you find the last lantern?" he asked, bemused. A delicate furrow graced the boy's white forehead for a few moments.

"There will always be another city."

And now the boy was here, his lips rather set, a satchel that certainly contained the lamp book swaying over his left shoulder. What had brought him up the flights of iron stairs, where each step might prompt second thoughts? Mystery? Curiosity? Hunger? As if feeding his pet lemur, the host turned to a bowl of smoked walnuts and proffered them. His young guest hesitated, then took a few, and stowed them in the pocket of his worn jacket.

Up to now, it had to be confessed, the predictions of the street seers had been mostly vapid and unexceptional. Marmoresh was not even sure he wanted to hear what they would say about his latest find. But he allowed Julian to pilot the boy towards the narrow-faced, thin, sallow prophet who liked to use the cards. In bored haste, but not without a sidelong glance at his benefactor for the night, this Max Vree shuffled the pack and then tautly placed the first seven face down. He looked up at Armand and asked him to uncover any three he liked. The boy did so as if he were simply following a lesson. There was no change in the features of his reader. "A journey by night. You will look deep into the other side of your soul. A moving fire, somehow. An echo in darkness. That is all." The boy stared at him and the fair down of his eyebrows was briefly ruffled.

A crone with a glass globe which she caressed with hands of mottled flesh was briefer still. "A blessing and a grace for you, from where you least expect it." Then she nodded sagely as if she had said a very portentous thing.

To his surprise, the next seer seemed almost as young as him: a sapling. Yet he was dashingly dressed: a white shirt stitched with fine lace, a red velvet jacket, sleek black trousers, and glinting, silver-buckled shoes. Armand felt abashed at the contrast with his own shabbiness. Julian murmured in his ear, "Here's the real thing. A tzigane." The brown boy took hold of his hand and he felt a shiver at the unfamiliar touch. Gently, the boy unfurled his fingers, and stretched them out so that the palm yearned towards him. He lowered his head towards the inscriptions in the flesh. Armand felt the sigh of his breath upon his outstretched skin. Then the boy looked up. "Your hand will hold the stone of heaven," he said, in a stark, simple way, as if it were a matter of no moment. He released Armand's hand and let the fingers spring back. Armand wanted to offer his palm again and ask him to read further, or simply to support the hand once more in that warm firm grasp. But the boy had moved quickly away. There was a murmur amongst the bystanders and a few questions were thrown towards the palmist, but he shook his head and folded his arms.

The young man who illustrated lamps felt an encircling arm guide him to stand before another in this curious fairground of fates. He stared at a dark-haired young woman, who reached forward and ran her hands through his hair. "Don't be afraid," she said, and he at once tightened his limbs and raised his face higher to look into her eyes. Her hands explored his face; they were cool and made him quiver inwardly. "I am Asphodel: and I only tell what the veil will allow. You . . . " There was a pause. He felt the green shadow of his mysterious patron, M. Marmoresh, fall upon him. The little lemur on a carved chair to one side of him whimpered for his master, holding out a claw. The girl-oracle called Asphodel shrugged. "You will see the end of all things."

Armand did not really register what happened after the last of these prophecies. He knew there was much chatter amongst his fellow guests and all sorts of remarks to him, some asking him what he thought they meant, some sceptically reassuring him that they could mean almost anything, others recalling what they had themselves been told, and a few offering him a shot of spirits and telling him the secret was to stay true, no matter what came, although true to what was not entirely clear. The master of the glass chamber merely regarded him from the marges of this throng and smiled softly, soothing the ruffled fur of his pet lemur, who also stared at him, with his owlish eyes.

By the time he left, he felt dizzy with the destinies he had been offered, and tried to remember them all, exactly as they were said, not just the words, but the manner; the card-reader's brusque summary, the orotund utterance of the crystal-gazer, the firm clench of the gypsy boy's hand and his breath upon his palm, and the eyes of Asphodel. He made his way carefully down the many stairs and opened wide the great arched door at the foot of the tower. He stepped out onto the gravel of the compound and then into the open ground surrounding it: below all the lights of the great city blazed. They seemed brittle and unusually bright, as if they were made of barley sugar. He wondered if the first of his fates would meet him soon.

Yet after these encounters, his days passed just as they had before. He woke in his room on Strelhov, hurriedly washed in the cold water, ate a husk of black bread, and went out to continue his book of all the lamps of the city, following the broader streets from the centre outwards, and then returning, as dusk began, on narrower byways which took more labyrinthine routes to the city's heart. He gave no attention to those he passed, and usually they gave none to him. Occasionally, a curious passer-by, usually a visitor, would ask to see what he was drawing, and he would politely but curtly oblige; some few would even ask if they might buy a sketch. He did not like to sell his work, but at night in his room, lit by the stub of a candle filched from a rich church, he would sometimes rapidly draw some pictures especially, and keep these pages in his satchel for just this purpose, for he needed the few crowns they earned. These depicted what he privately thought of as the high lanterns of the city, those that by their grandeur or significance drew people's attention more than the others:

a pair, with their vast prismatic glass cases, upon the Great Bridge, one, festooned with the royal and imperial eagles in gilt at the gateway to the Castle, one—many-forked and cascading with ornament—in the centre of the Old Square, and another, simple and stark and leaning at a slight angle, in the bend of the cobbled road of the Street of Chroniclers.

Still such days followed one by one and stretched ahead, and he saw no sign of what he had been told would befall him. He was sometimes filled with a bitter dreariness, as if he were a gutter weed that had been uprooted, briefly planted amongst the rich soil of the pampered orchids, fed, fêted and bathed in warmth, promised greater things yet, and then abruptly banished to the gutter again. True, invitation cards occasionally arrived from Simon Marmoresh, but he spurned them. He felt he had been duped, made a plaything. No doubt the master in his tower looked down below and laughed. Maybe his blasé guests implored him to summon back the entertaining child with the threadbare satchel, so that they could scoff again. Even the lemur's gibberings echoed in his ears as if in mockery.

When calmer, he reflected that nevertheless the episode had given him some things: the grip of the gypsy boy's hand, the fine fleeting fingers of Asphodel in his hair and upon his face, the flattering attention of the coterie, even, he ruefully thought as he gnawed at his rough bread, a handful of smoked walnuts. Once, he thought he caught sight of another of the guests on that night of prophecy, and sometimes he wondered if the seemingly chance strangers who asked after his pictures were really charitable emissaries sent by Marmoresh in this guise. These purchasers, whoever they were, kept him in a bare existence but no more, and they did not change his days.

Since he had first come to the city, at fifteen, with the little money salved from the sale of the few goods left in his parents' looted rooms, he had seen the street lights as his staunchest friends. He had counted them in that way when he roamed the streets at night, reckoning the paces between them, pausing beneath their welcoming corona, and placing his shoulders against them for support. He liked to imagine how they would still be there when all else was gone. At night, then, he saw the darkened lamp-posts sway in dance as the fierce winds of the ruined world roared, heard them hum songs they learned from the stars, and wondered if they would ever dream of those who had passed beneath their gleaming lights long ago.

But now even such signal friends seemed scarcely enough to sustain his spirits, and he was both cast down and yet secretly hopeful when, as if by chance, he met in the street Max Vree, who caught him by his worn sleeve.

"I have a message for you, young man."

"From Marmoresh? I don't . . . "

"Just a message. Why don't you try to look at what lies *below* the lamps?"

Armand frowned and caught his breath as if to reply, but the thin prophet had gone. "What lies below?" Slumped, drunken tramps and the leavings of dogs, flapping trapped newspapers, grey street pigeons, spent matches. What else? He tramped on, more dejected still.

By the end of the day he felt he had never been so weary. But he was unwilling to contemplate returning to the cold narrow cell of his room, preferring even the dank October chill to that. Besides, he had, at the last, made a sale of a number of his "souvenir" pictures all together, and was quite in pocket for once. He decided not to harbour the money carefully, and gave himself the luxury of wondering what to do with it. As he approached the edge of the Old Square, he heard a shoe-shine boy still shouting his trade, and he glanced down at his own atrociously shoddy shoes. With a sigh, he slumped onto the high-backed folding chair at the boy's pitch beneath a light, and said, "I don't know what you will be able to do with these." The urchin grinned, gently pulled his right foot towards him, rested it on a sloping stool, and began to flourish the tools of his craft—brush, cloth, polish, cloth, brush, and then the same with his left foot, all with deft ease. Then he stepped back to admire his handiwork. "There: you can see your face in them now."

He took hold of the sole of Armand's shoe and tilted it upwards towards his client. As if it might really be true, Armand looked down. And indeed he fancied he did see, in the black patina, a dark mirror image of a troubled young face, as if in the ripples of a deep secret pool: a tousled Narcissus gazing back at him. He passed his tongue over his lips. Why should this face look so careworn? With a light leap, he descended from the form, and rewarded the boy. Their hands met as the coins passed between them. Admiring the burnished shoes, Armand walked on, without noticing much where he was going.

As the day grew more dim, he found himself in the passage-way that ran past the side of Saint Casimir's: and in a narrow porch of the church he saw an old woman standing. She was wrapped in a folded headscarf, floral frock and what seemed numerous aprons. Her pale blue eyes had a strange staring film over them and Armand guessed that she was half-blind. Her head moved very slightly, almost imperceptibly, at the sound of his footsteps. She neither put out a hollow hand nor said any beseeching words, but nevertheless Armand approached, took her withered claw in his and placed there some coins, closing the stubborn fingers upon them. These swiftly placed the gift in an apron pocket; and in return the old woman begged the blessings of Saint Casimir to fall upon him.

He saw ahead the gate of the Perennial Park, where ever-greens and winter-flowering shrubs were nurtured to offer the people of the city a pleasing refuge all year long: but it was a favourite, too, in the warmer months because of its open spaces, benches and secluded walkways. Just inside, beneath the modest entrance lamp on its green-painted column, there was a brass drinking-fountain. Armand advanced towards it and was about to bow down and take a drink when his eyes met an old veteran with the same thought in mind. At once, he straightened and deferred to the silver-jowled, crooked ancient. But he in turn gestured Armand to go first. The young man smiled and opened his hand to invite the older to have precedence, but he inclined his head and nodded that he would like to give way. There they stood for quite a minute or two, nodding, smiling and bowing at each other—and neither getting a drink—until the absurdity caught them both at once and they both burst into grins. Armand shrugged and put his head down to the spout, with its coat of verdigris. The water tasted better than ever as he tried to catch it in between his laughing lips. He rose up and thanked the old man again, and for a moment they both enjoyed this little complicity. The grizzled reprobate in his creased shirt and greasy suit waved his battered straw hat at him as he went on his way.

Within the gardens, all was cool and shaded, and the October dusk was flying its pennons of grey and twilight blue among the tall trees. Absorbed in the gloom, Armand heard a rumbling noise and caught on the air a familiar smell he could not at once place. His memory briefly lunged back to the Moravian town of his childhood and an evening like this, quiet, fading, but somehow filled with a quick joy. Then he saw through the trees a red glow, a bright blaze, gliding steadily, as if a giant carried a lantern of coal. He stood still while he watched the approaching fiery apparition as it snaked along the winding path towards him, and he snuffed the sharp, warm, slightly acrid fumes, and searched for the lost recollection from his days at home.

Then there emerged through the passage, in a grove of cypress trees just ahead, a chestnut seller with his glowing cart, and the waft of his wares hit the young man with full force. And he remembered how just such a fiery vessel had entranced him as a child, and his father had bought a bag to share, and carefully peeled the husks and blown upon the kernels while he, imploring, had held up his hand for them. Armand nodded at the seller and said he had just what he needed. "You're in luck," he replied, "It's the last of the day, so I'll give you a lot more." And he shovelled the chestnuts, some with a coating of ash, some still faintly glowing, into a black waxed-paper bag, just like the one Armand remembered his father holding above him. Gratefully, the boy gave up his coin and, with a few more words, watched the humble alembic wheel away.

Then, with scorched fingertips and greedy glee, he took the secret fiery fruit away to a bench to eat.

When the creaking of the wheels of the chestnut-seller's cart faded into the distance, a silence fell. On his bench, he leant back luxuriously and looked again at his polished shoes, raising the sole from the floor and resting on his heels. He let his gaze wander over the shadowy vistas of the park. Dark birds wheeled overhead, cawing. The dusk was now almost palpable, a fine mesh made of cobwebs and dust which veiled the trees and paths and grass in a grey glamour. He thought it might be time to tramp back to his room before the park gates were closed and locked: but he felt too a strange reluctance to leave. Undecided, and still enjoying the tingling the chestnuts had left upon his fingers and the warmth in his taut belly, he simply rested and stared.

And then he heard a high chanting, a girl's sing-song voice reciting a rhyme, and descried below, in a little sheltered grove, a glimmering of white, just beneath the diffused amber glow of a solitary lamp. Armand was not at all sure that he had this lamp in his collection—he had not been so far into the park before and did not really know there was one here: so, clutching his satchel, he made his way cautiously towards it. But as he drew near, his gaze shifted from the lost lamp to the figure that danced in its wan light.

She was, he thought, about his own age. She wore a simple white muslin dress tied in the middle with a pale blue sash. Pale hair cascaded from a straw hat and the light caught it in glinting filaments. And she was jumping, stooping, then leaping again, upon a pattern of squares chalked upon the asphalt. Armand approached more stealthily; she had not heard him yet. Her white shape, her strange movements, the secrecy of the sheltered dell, the gray haze of the dusk and the shimmering light, all affected him deeply, and he felt he could only gaze upon them. But then she reached the end of the pattern, and quickly twisted around to return, and saw him; and he sensed her quick intake of breath. There was a brittle silence, broken only by the serrated croak of an old jackdaw in the bruised sky. Armand nodded at her and waved a hand, and she paused: but then she bent to the ground again with a sure grace, he saw her fingers flicker, and she straightened, and with a few more deft strides and movements danced towards him, and regarded him solemnly.

"They tell me I am too old for this now, you see," she confided, without any preamble, or even greeting. "So I have to sneak away and play in secret."

He nodded, and suddenly was glad his shoes had been polished. "Will you show me?" he ventured, surprised at his own boldness.

She shook her head. "But you can watch—again," she added, with a little twist of her mouth. And suddenly once more there was a flurry of white and with a grave grace she danced her rite, there and back again. He saw her throw a red pebble onto the pattern, and leap on the square where it landed, then once more and again, first on one foot, then on two, and in particular he saw how she avoided in her prancing an oblong near the end which was shown in thicker chalk and gaped like an open maw. While she rested, and looked upon him with amusement, he examined more carefully the forms she had marked out, particularly the penultimate niche. A laugh came after his doubled-up shape.

"Careful—you are about to step into hell!"

He turned quickly and almost overbalanced.

"What?"

"At the end, you must leap over the mouth of hell and land in heaven, the last square. That's the way it always is."

And she rose to her feet, threw her pebble with a deft flick, and danced once more her measure, coming to rest in the celestial realm, next to where he stood, outside the pattern. They regarded each other for a few moments.

Then she let out her breath quickly and started back, and he saw a little spiral of chalk rise up in a sudden puff, and she was withdrawing the sole of her shoe from where it had quickly touched the forbidden ground. A great creaking complaint came from a bird overhead. She steadied herself and tried to assume a careless smile.

"Perhaps they are right. I shouldn't be playing these games, particularly at night. They'll be closing the gates soon, and I must be off. Or I won't be allowed back again." And, holding her hat on her head, she fled, in a scramble of rippling white.

Armand watched her go, wistfully, reflecting on the exact balance of her last words and how well he was meant to note the promise of return. Then he bent to look at what had startled her. Where she had stood, in the last square, was a roughly rounded piece of quartz, the scintillant mineral the jackdaws loved to hoard. He tilted it to the light and saw it glint: there was a thin green vein running through it, as if of fossilised moss, a primeval relic. Thoughtfully, he put the shining pebble in his pocket, where it rested against the empty shell of the last of the smoked walnuts, which he had whimsically preserved.

It was difficult to see any distance ahead now, and though he did not want to leave the strange domain that the park had become, he thought he must try to make his way to its boundary wall and follow this around until he came to a gate. And so he strolled on, pensively, relishing to himself all that had passed; the dusk, the dance, the taste of the chestnuts, the little courtesies at the brass fountain, the old woman's murmured blessing, the eagerness of the shoe shine boy, and then again the seemly grace of the girl and her game, and the sudden gift from the quarrelsome jackdaws, that glinting orb of quartz.

Through the gloom ahead he saw the sharper mass of a low roof, and he quickened his stride towards it. As he approached, he saw a crimson ember hover in the air; nearer still, and this resolved itself into the glowing end of a pipe stuck in the contented mouth of a whiskered man in the sward-green uniform of the parkmen. He asked if he was too late to leave by the nearest gate, and the elder man thoughtfully removed his pipe and said he was too late for them all; "curfew fell a few minutes ago."

"But step inside," he added.

Armand lowered his head as he followed onto the stone-flagged floor of the pavilion, where there were a few bare items—a chair, a couch, an ancient stove, a mildewed bookcase, and a table heaped with leaves.

"You are lucky to find me here, in fact," the fellow continued, "I am only so to speak a spare, the autumn keeper they call me, they bring me in to help sweep up the leaves, you see? The rest of the time this place is shuttered up and so you would have found it empty. You should smell the must when I first open it up. *Wheesh.* And it never really goes. You can get it now, I don't doubt."

The young man snuffed dutifully and nodded.

"Well, kind sir, it is like this. I am not supposed to let anyone in or out after the gates are closed, not even the Emperor himself, if he should call here—"

And then he seemed to remember that there was no Emperor any more, or so they said, and so he added, more vaguely, "or anyone of that kind. Now you might think a small consideration would solve that little matter . . . "— here he looked archly at Armand under thick peppery eyebrows—"but no, you see, and for why? Because I am not allowed to accept perquisites neither."

Armand nodded. "Well, then, if you would be so kind, what if I were to stay here?"

The autumn keeper took another draw of his pipe and exhaled, and Armand wondered if it were not after all the curious fumes from this that contributed to the pavilion's atmosphere.

"Charmed, I am sure, sir, charmed. Yet there is another way. I cannot accept gifts, but let us suppose you wanted to buy something from me. Anyone can see the difference. You might have come here expressly to buy such a thing, and so naturally I would let you in and out as if you were simply a visitor of mine, do you see?"

The young man looked about.

"Many people," the pipe-illumined park keeper continued, "take a fancy to my books."

"Your books?"

"Here," and the keeper unearthed from the pile upon the table what looked like a handful of autumn sweepings.

"I choose the finest ones, you see, and I sew them together. Look . . . "

With a few swift movements, he gathered up a dozen of so of the scarlet, amber, copper and umber leaves, though not with any noticeable finesse of judgement, and ran a silver needle with rough black thread through them, biting off the cord at the end and making a quick neat knot. He handed the result to Armand, who turned the brittle, mottled pages carefully. He looked at the striations and markings upon each leaf as if he were reading maps in a strange atlas, and he reflected that as the days passed, probably the pages would change too, in ways he could not foresee. He certainly wanted this book, and would have, even if it were not also the key to the world beyond.

He paid the autumn keeper his fee, and the old man pocketed this gratefully. At the last, as they stood by the gate, a pang of conscience seemed to assail him.

"Mind, the book will fade and fall away in the end, you understand. That always happens. But there's plenty to look at and enjoy in the meantime."

Armand said solemnly that he understood.

High on Petrin Hill, Simon Marmoresh gazed upon the last lights of the city below. He fed his lemur Timoleon another slice of medlar, and the creature took it with fastidious care. A fragrance of sweet decay came from the autumn fruit, and played in the air.

The Amber Cigarette

A silver cigarette case, slim as a sword's face, and engraved with radiating lines, like a stylised sunrise: and the sun was a gem of jasper. It would do very well for his favourite brand, those delicate tapers of amber paper made only by Desmay. Inside was a couch of green sarsenet where they would nestle restfully.

"Each case is made only once, sir," the young man said. He had fair hair, and a brittle stare, as if his eyes were made of crushed glass. The collector Ivor Seymour looked at the design again. How fine the filigree of the rays, as if light had been made tangible. The silversmith had incised the lines as delicately as a leaf-fossil. And the crimson stone was marked with strange veins.

"It is said the gem is Alexandrian," the boy offered, diffidently. His customer looked up—steadily, so as not to show undue eagerness.

"Said?"

The youth adjusted his left shirt cuff, a shining white band.

"We cannot exactly state the provenance. But its cut, and its character, suggest that to us."

"I see." He was secretly amused by the lofty wisdom, worldly yet rarefied, that the young man affected.

The case must be his, to possess and to caress, so that his touch might traverse the scriven filaments and his eye gaze often upon the curious stone. He would own it. He nodded.

The boy covered the case in black waxed paper and fastened the parcel in straw-coloured string.

After the dimness inside, light streamed in the streets, and his eyelids faltered. He turned back once: on the drawn blinds, the assistant's silhouette was still, a statue made of grey shade.

He kept the case in its dark veils for several days: he dare not look upon it. But his fingers found the little sable-coated packet often, and they longed to release the coarse golden cords.

He chose a day when clouds of umber squatted in the sky, and a dead gloom had descended upon his room. He felt out a solution to the locks of the knots the young man had made, and released the wrappings. The sliver of silver slipped from its sheath of shadow and shone like a shivering stream: and the stone stared at him. It was an amulet, he was sure: and it held within its red heart a serpentry of secrets, if only he could read its old chalcedony tongue.

He looked hard at the markings on the polished jasper and they almost seemed to form shapes, which, however, did not quite cohere, were always elusive. He thought of a cabinet of wax seals he had once seen, gouts of scarlet bearing creatures impressed upon them: sea-goats, gorgetted swans, staring gorgons, long-tongued lions, snorting wyverns, crowned ravens. He expected the stone, if he looked long enough, to yield up just such a beast, but perhaps one never known or seen before.

He pressed the lip to release the lid, took a handful of the Desmay cigarettes from an onyx box, and placed them one by one upon the green silk cushion within. Then he snapped the case shut and gazed again at the design on its face. This time it was the silver rays that drew him to them. The starved light of his room seemed to concentrate itself upon the gleaming veneer, so that a bloom arose upon it and the delicate lines were all illuminate. They even seemed to

extend themselves beyond the case and continue into the dark
air. For a moment the fancy took him that he could follow
their path: that perhaps a subtle engraver might have the skill
to extend his craft even unto the aether. He dwelt upon the
idea, then dismissed it. He lit one of the amber cigarettes:
it was exquisite upon his lips, and the fumes possessed his
breath in an insidious embrace until he released them into
the dull room with a long, slow sigh.

The pale fumes, tinted with lavender, coiled and uncoiled
in a languorous slow ballet as if they were his dreaming
thoughts made visible. Through this fine haze he allowed his
gaze to alight upon the treasures of his chamber, while his
fingers still plied upon the cigarette case, delicately sensing
the chased striations and lingering over the japer gem, the
red parhelion, as if they might draw out by their very touch
the creature that had its lair within.

In a niche, a white hollow in the walls of his room, there
was a statuette of Venus enmeshed, and he saw how the tracery
of the net which harnessed the marble form of the goddess
was carven with the same care and precision as the rays upon
his silver case, frail and austere as cobwebs in frost. It was as
if both artists, the sculptor and the silversmith, had seen and
understood the same apparition of ethereal threadwork, the
same touchless fibres. Through the veil of the spiralling incense
of his cigarette, he looked also at the mask of Antinous-Osiris,
suspended in a high place with its dark sightless eye sockets.
The boy-god wore the hierurgic headdress of the Egyptian
deity and its linear folds, like stone wings, were etched with
a rare definition and purity. They emanated from a radiant
brooch at the boy's brow. Its creator had certainly known the
secret of this sun and the light that led from it.

Some shifting in the clouds outside released a wan shaft
of sunlight through the tall windows, and in its feeble glow
he saw a ceremony of dust motes, each a minute jewel,

each moving to its own fervid purpose, like the acolytes of a Dionysian ritual. It came to him that all the seemingly solid objects of his room were in reality as impalpable as these, that in their inner essence they too cavorted to a wild measure, were each a frozen dance. That lacquered escritoire, embellished with peacocks and cranes, might have a will to strut and posture like the birds depicted upon its surface: that eighteenth century walnut chair, with clawed feet, might want to mimic the fabulous beast whose paws it possessed; that poker of twisted brass could harbour the urge to untwist its tortured metal, and its gleaming head might swivel to glare at those who dared to touch it.

Suppose, too, that the volumes on his shelves should decide to descend into human form? That frail white vellum folio of Iamblichus with gilt devices, might it not become a fragile youth whose pale flesh still harboured embellishments of gold? The book of sultry verses bound in blue morocco could become a creature whose azure flesh rippled with strange delights, while that stout quarto of the *Complete Works of Tobias Crisp*, the seventeenth century libertine divine, might make itself a great rollicking figure with a sly gaze. Their talk would be all of the words within them, and the choice phrases and arcane ideas would swirl in the air like sprites unleashed from some ancient spellbound captivity.

And what if it were possible that some mortals possessed the same secret? What if there were some—it surely could not be all—who were able to divest themselves of their flesh at will and take on a new form whenever they chose? Surely that was the hidden meaning behind the story of the Fall. Originally, perhaps, all potentialities, human, natural, animal, existed together in constant flux and mutability, fluid, unseparate. It was only the descent into matter that had ended this, that had congealed the contents of the athanor, fixing them each in one distinct, dreadful, deadened form.

As he gazed again upon the curious veins in the cabochon of jasper, as the whorls of his fingertips still played upon the silver rays that emanated from it, he wondered if some adept, armed with the requisite talisman, might find again that fluid world where all is a constant re-shaping and restless change, where there would be forms, spirits, unities, comminglings, that have no equivalent on earth, where there are beings not human, not animal, not natural, but utterly inconceivable to us. He thought of the old tales of metamorphosis, of the youth in the tale of Apuleius who had betrayed the Mysteries and whose comely, precious form was changed to that of an ass, and could not be restored until he ate ceremonial roses. Surely here were hints; but they were indeed only half-truths. The adept knew, he suspected, that the true transformation was not into one form only, but to gain the ability to undergo constant change, to become all creatures, all created things: and any hybrid of these.

Yet how to unlock the flesh to enter this realm of infinite experience? He extinguished his cigarette in a shallow jade bowl, and the last of its emanations were gradually diffused into the dim air of the room. For a long time he remained as he was, in a state of abstraction, while his hand still caressed the silver cigarette case. The fumes had made him drowsy and remote from diurnal things. He felt as though there was some subtle, elliptical step he could take, a slight shifting of his mind, which would take him into a different state of being altogether. But he knew that if he made a lunge towards this, if he put his focus upon it too directly, the door would disappear. It could only be approached by a process akin to the knight's move in chess, at once angular and linear. Until he could make that move, he allowed his thoughts to drift lazily like the last ghosts of the lavender smoke of the cigarette, still lingering in the further cornices and recesses of his chamber.

He thought of the young man who had so tactfully whetted his interest in the cigarette case. He had not been garrulous in his praises, or urgent in pressing its qualities. He had simply selected the two most important characteristics, shrewdly judging the tastes and prejudices of this collector. The piece was unique: and probably its gem was ancient, was from a city whose reputation for arcane wisdom was legendary. Those facts had been quite enough to fortify Seymour in his desire to own the piece. And then there was the deft care with which the youth had veiled the shining object in sombre cerements, so that it still kept its aura of mystery until it left his hands. Certainly, then, there was an art and a grace even in the work of a shopkeeper's assistant: if, indeed, that is all the boy was. He thought of the crushed glaze of his eyes, and wondered.

His fingers had not left the thing he had purchased, and now he brought it up closer to his eyes. The clouded day had shifted imperceptibly into the onset of dusk, and the pall that had hardly left his room was now strengthened. It seemed to him, too, that the darkness must behave as the dust motes did, must be an active, restless concentration of particles, black crystals that danced as they defied the light. And if that were so, perhaps all things possessed those sinister sparkling shards too, so that his books, the peacock escritoire, the taloned chair, the contorted poker, had it in them to become things of uttermost sin.

He stared again at the sphere of worked jasper. The serpentine veins seemed to writhe before him, making and unmaking themselves in roiling figures. His eyelids flickered. And then as he watched, he saw that the lineaments of the stone were himself transformed: the shapes he could see were his own. And as he regarded these strange creatures, it was as if his soul traversed the radiating lines that shone from the stone, as if it soared into an unknown empyrean. Then he knew that its journey was towards a form in the void, a vast figure, all still and silent: a statue made of shade.

The Ka of Astarakhan

S ince the decree of 1906, we are now allowed to count the cawing of the crows, and even to make predictions from them. Such freedom! And do you know what they are saying, what they foretell? *Raark, raark!* There is a black time coming, that's what they say. All the birds bring prophecies, if we only heeded their languages.

The painter Pyotr has brought me here to this derelict bath-house, in an abandoned little spa, somewhere in the middle of the country. I don't know exactly where, except that it is still far from Astrakhan. I am on a journey to Astrakhan, the city on the estuary, where the Volga lets its veins out to the sea. The Khan, the Sultan and the Tsar all tried in their turn to possess this city: they all kissed ashes. It belongs to houris and demi-gods, krakens and marsh-monsters.

The villagers let me lie here out of pity. They do not know my past. Some fevered ex-soldier, perhaps. That is true. But they would be surprised to find, too, that I was once the King of Time, the President of the World, the Grand Tabulator of History, the Archon of the Stars. Yet all these things indeed I have been, and now I am after all the *Ka of Astarakhan*, and that is a city which will go where it likes, under and beyond the heavens, and it is a city of infinite riches.

There is mildew on my lungs and cold beads form upon my skin. They mop them away for me, but they come again. Translucent, they might form the diadem for an angel, but instead they are soaked into an unclean grey cloth. The hair sticks to my forehead, a brow where men once read signs. Perhaps this is to mask or veil whatever is forming there, for it is too terrible to know.

The bath house has echoes. On the wall there are two hollow iron troughs, which have a green scum to them and are streaked with spittles of white. They give off whispers. The livid rime will live long when all else is gone.

I should have gone to Montenegro that year—1910? 1910!—a propitious year—when it became a kingdom. I remember I met a cadet of the royal house in Petropolis where he had been sent for schooling. He told me of the white mountains—they are not black—of his home and in turn I told him how this little realm could become the first futurian state of Europe. We plotted how we would discover all the other waves there are in the air besides radio: how its towns could be washed with tides of scent, taste, spirit, dreams.

But if I had gone to Montenegro, I might never have found my way to Astarakhan. No, I have not got that wrong. *Astara*khan. Long ago I was able to show how all history could be changed by simply altering one of our old words, by placing an extra letter just so in the middle of it, or come to that at its beginning or end. That stray character, that interloper, moves the flow of the word within the world and makes a subtle shift in all our meanings. Moreover, a word does not lose its power just because people do not understand it.

So, there is the city of my childhood, Astrakhan so close so far from the Caspian shore, Astrakhan of the warehouses and the wharves, Astrakhan the capital of tobacco and the queen of pomegranates. And there is the city I have conjured up by the simple intercession of a single letter: Astarakhan. That is a city at the vanguard of a new science, a curious art. You will need it in the future: you will need it to make the future.

Yellow stars sing in my eyes.

What is astrology! The science and art of the influence of
the planets and stars upon human behaviour. Precisely. Well,
what about the reverse? Why shouldn't humans influence
the planets and stars? I have called this Astarology. I am
convinced it can be done. We will move the influence of a
constellation so as to leave a void in the heavens and into this
we will stream our dreams. The zodiac shivers! We shall stare
at the stars and see them blink, just for an instant. Chance
and caprice will be at last at large in the universe, fleas in the
fur of that beast's fixed destinies.

Astarakhan is the first astarological city. And I am its ka.
The ka? The ka is in the word of the city and its spirit. While
the old city lolls upon its slow lapping waters, its ka goes
out into the void. Summoned in me, summed up in me,
it visits all aeons and all gulphs. The dome of the ascension
is in my head, its minarets are in my fingers, its Kalmyk
prayer-wheels revolve in my eyes, its five-pointed star is on
my forehead. There are wings of blue and silver at my heels
and shoulder-blades. As I soar through the heavens, I pass
the vessels and steeds of the great deities: the astral chariots,
palanquins, chargers, arks, boats, clouds, citadels, carpets,
stars, panthers, all in their high and holy heraldry. And I
see the constellations reel, and the fiery comets rise in the
black skies.

But my body still lies here upon its pallet with a sullen
pillow at its head. They have brought herbs to strew around
me to drive away the fever. The stalks are sharp on my flesh
and the scent of the dark serrated leaves is bitter. Sometimes
when they come to tend to me, I see surprise blaze in their
solemn gaze: I think they have caught a glimpse of me in my
transfigured form, I think in the corner of their eyes they
might have caught the flicker of a wing-beat.

The arches of my ribs are clearly to be seen when I lift
my head to look at my body. They are white arches, like the

architecture of some fine future city of light, all curves and clean geometry. I see the arches spring from the streets in graceful parabolas. I see them soar to the freed sky, and the minds of the people soar with them. And my feet, with their upright towers of bone, signal the tall structures that the new cities will own, where the people will live when their hovels and shacks have all been swept away. Even my own body, you see, is a blueprint for the future.

And also an amulet of the past. When I roll my eyeballs upward, which is painful, like a moving bruise, I see the shaggy overhang of my dark eyebrows. They are like twin scarab-beetles gathering the black moss of my thoughts from my brow. That black moss is a precious substance.

Perhaps on the wall they are not just iron tubs. Perhaps they are the gongs of Mars. I made all my friends Martians, I remember. Freed from being Earth people, we proclaimed new possibilities. We told the Tsar about it. He did not reply. Later, we pretended to be simple removal men and rang the Winter Palace to ask when we should come to take everything away, since the occupants, we had heard, would soon be moving out. The court official took the joke in good part: perhaps he was afraid to do anything other. But it was not only a joke. For I had cast the tables, and I knew when the revolution would come. Yes, for a while I was held in a certain awe at the accuracy of my prediction. But they did not want to know quite how I had worked it out, did not want to see the sway and dance of the numbers across the aeons that I had discovered.

And so here I am, in a rackety bath house. Fat men came here once to cleanse and baste their bodies. The pine walls, along with the wood's own sweet resin, must be slick with their residues, their flayings, their unction, all that oozed from them. This shall be my chrism then. Armed with such essence, what basilisk or cockatrice could ever defy me?

As I cannot move, I have to watch for what moves around me. Through the dust-covered window-pane and the cracks of the walls there are fissures of sunlight and later the tattered strips of darkness.

It is easy to see the secret words that have led me to lie here in a simple low-pitched bath house with its grove of birch trees. Here I am no more than a house of breath and hardly even that. It is a few twists of the alphabet to a dearth of breath, and we do not need to say what follows that. Then, I will lie in a house of earth. There is a missing word between bath, breath, dearth, and earth, and I do not dare breathe it. But it lingers in the weak sunlight and in the tattered dark.

When after the revolution wild-haired Wassily K. started his Institute for Artistic Culture—what a phrase! —I had no choice but to retort with an Institute for Antarctic Culture. And such culture, in a land where no man lives! What fine pure white sculpture, what howling sea-wind symphonies, what vast nude unwritten books, what ballets of undisturbed birds! However, I was wrong. I have been giving it much thought. The Antarctic, after all, is a giant white clock-face at the end of the world. Once it had very slow black hands that told a geological time. We can no longer see them. Where have the black hands gone?

I think they may be upon me, at my throat.

This Ka of Astarakhan is becoming rarer still, barely a breath, a scent, an air, no more: soon I will become the Attar of Astarakhan, all its essence purged and macerated into its frailest possible form, all its marshy morass of myth and history distilled so that it is but a zephyr of faintest fragrance. Ivan and Tamurlane and Osman, you wanted this great city? Here it is, less than a feather, a freshet, a fever, a shiver.

I thought once that at this time there would be an inrush of meaning. All else winnowed away, I would at last be able to say: this is the essence. It is not so. But instead, pictures flicker in and out of view. With my brother Aleskandr in the Ural Mountains, watching the flight paths of birds across the translucent amber of the dawn sky, as if we were reading moving hieroglyphs. Seeing the fatal numbers tumble into place in my study on the Caspian shore as the oil wells burnt and sent black plumes and scarlet tongues into the sky: as if my arithmetic and this apocalypse were pitching against each other in a mad mazurka. The night that I lay on Persian sands where a strange horned beetle made its home in my hair as I slept, and seemed to whisper secrets, so that I awoke relucent and envisioned. And my days as a boy among the nomads, inhaling the rank perfume of their dung-fires, hearing the tingling of their ancestral camel-bells, tasting the sour-milk tea they served in leather cups, watching their veiled young women light candles at stone shrines, and knowing upon my skin the fretful touch of the winds—who is this? who is this?—come with us, come with us, go on further.

Seeing that I am scarcely here, Pyotr, poor fellow, becomes worried and leans over to stare. He asks what he can get me. I sigh, and say:

"A Ziggurat cigarette."

"A Ziggurat . . . ?"

And then he remembers. An idea of my own, that in the future people will be able to smoke cigarettes made of the upper air. They will light up tubes of aether, tapers of cerulean essence. Tell me more about the future, he says, watching me with his sorrowful eyes. It is to distract me, I know.

I have set it all out in my Tablets of Fate, according to the strictest, most fiendishly difficult algebra that only I so far have ever mastered. This work, which made clear the fortunes of peoples and nations, did not get the reception it deserved. Yet strangely even those who sneered most at my mathematical formulae predicting the passage of kalpas were still anxious to hear my views on the most imminent matters and on their own destiny. They did not believe in my precise science: yet they longed for the touch of my simple mystique. That is how it is with us. I humoured them. So, now, for Pyotr:

"In the future there will be shops of shadows," I say, "where you can choose your own dark companion. Why have only one, that mimics you? Try this one, sir, with pointed ears, or this with a forked tail; or, madam, would you like yours winged? You, commissioner, you are perhaps a little rounder than you wish? Here is a svelte shadow for you. General, you would rather be an obelisk than a barrel? It can be done. You, young poet, you have lost your lover? We can fashion a shadow in her guise, she will accompany you always. And never any crying either."

"What else?"

"What else? This is not enough? Very well! Then there will also be bazaars full of reflections where you can ask for the mirror image of your secret desires. It will be you, yet a changed you. A touch more distinction around the temples, my dear sir: a hint more coral flesh in the lips, madam; and you, leader of the workers, more steel and coal in the eyes, perhaps? Glittering silver slivers, black spectres, carry them home over your arm, and try them out in private."

But why all this babble of shops? Here they do not even have food. And I could not eat it if they did. I asked in jest for the black tea of Muscovy. The old babushka waddled away, muttering, and brought me some brackish water. Something, even in these times, makes her still give kindness to a stranger. What is that? There is nothing I can give her except the blessing of a prophet. Perhaps that is all that she wants. She cut a lock from my hair last night when she thought I was asleep. After all, she may not be wrong. When I went to Persia, they called me a Russian dervish and a wandering saint, an orchid-priest. And when I proclaimed the Book in

Baku, that is the Book of Oceans and Stars, even schoolboys put down their pastry cakes and listened open-mouthed.

It was not always so. In the metropolis they said that I murmured or purred my poems and even when they could be heard they could not be understood. Cafés and cabarets emptied when I appeared, or else the chatter and the clatter of dishes got louder. Then, some practical jokers in Kharkov got me into a theatre to proclaim me President of the Globe, sneering behind their pale hands. I took my oath solemnly: they would have been more solemn too, if they could see what I could learn from the lines of their white palms. And when I have been forced to walk in the streets in sandals and rags, they have stoned me and shouted words harder than stones too. This is never advisable. How do you ever know who is among you?

In the city on the delta of my long ago days there were forty churches of the old faith, five of the Armenian, two of the Latin and one of the Lutheran: also there were three Turkish mosques, one Persian, one Azeri, two synagogues and a Buddhist prayer-house. And there were other temples and shrines of saints who changed their shapes along with their worshippers. Despite this, still the gods escaped. They were easily discerned in the dusty streets and the squares. Olive-hued strangers, with almondine eyes, never quite fully seen, not absolutely in focus. Children chalked their images in strokes and circles: their faces glinted in the shuttle of the beads plied by old walnut-faced women; and their forms foamed in the play of the caliph's fountain.

I have nothing now, but I have owned precious things. A poet gave me a tie of twilight grey. I had a silver salt dish, encrusted with verdigris. I carved a pen from a willow twig. With the goblin K., I made a pack of devil's playing cards. And everywhere I went I shed paper, paper, as a serpent relinquishes its skin. There might have been writing, or drawing, or equations, or diagrams on those shreds: there might have been only the signs of the snake's writhing. One day they will surely issue my *Collected Writhings*. And they will gather what is left of my possessions for a museum. The King of the Future touched these! Please, do not touch, no, do not taint, do not let these lose their lustre. The *Ka of Astarakhan* once spread his wings over these relics.

Pyotr wants me to write out something. He has placed a sheet of paper in my hands, where it moves of its own accord. If you hold a sheet of brittle paper in both hands and let it ripple, or if, as now, the paper moves itself, it will crackle like flames, like white flames. It is like listening to a fire. Is not that the true elemental language of the paper? Why put words upon it, after all? Just listen. *Crackle, crackle, crack, flicker, ripple, rip, rackle, rackle, rack, rack, raark, raark.*

I can feel fingers of light on my eyelids.

My throat no longer speaks to my chest.

I can hear the rasping of the last language upon my tongue. *Raark, raark.*

The Original Light

My Uncle Vasta made small bunches of flowers from the weeds and wild blooms that grew in the abandoned gardens of our town. Each day he would walk around a particular quarter in turn, trying to sell them for a few pennies at the door, until they were all gone or had dropped their heads in shame when they were shunned. I do not know if my uncle had ever had any other trade. But he had certainly always had other studies. Into each bouquet, held together by twists of wire or string or even shoelaces that he found in the street, and sheathed in a newspaper cone, he would insert a little slip of yellow paper with a handwritten prophecy. He sometimes said that the more superstitious housemaids or landladies who kept the houses where he called were as willing to buy his clumps of flowers for the pieces of fortune inside as for the charm of the blooms he had chosen.

He therefore gave a great deal of thought in the evenings, seated in his shawl at the table, to what he would write upon these flimsy talismans. He would sometimes study almanacs for phrases, not in order to copy them, but so that he understood the shape of a prophecy, and then his brittle blue eyes would become thoughtful and after a while his fingers, on which the earth of the wild garden plots had long ago etched a grimy ineradicable map, would slowly transcribe a few arrowed words with his dip-pen, in a whorl of dark ink. Each one, and on this he prided himself, was different, even if some were more curious than others. I am sure his proverbs and predictions were indeed liked, even if abashedly, by the women who were good enough to give him a few small coins for his posies. But this might also have been because my uncle always took care with his appearance. Certainly his silvered suit was aged, but it was well brushed, and still had its waistcoat which made my uncle look all the more respectable, and he had four woollen ties, in rust, moss, ochre and mushroom colours, that he knotted into an extravagant flourish. He had a neat dark moustache, like well-schooled handwriting, and long cheek-bones that tautened his olive skin, and gave him an almost austere look. So he did not seem like some wild prophet but rather a fallen gentleman whose word, and whose omens, might be trusted.

Winter itself did not deter my uncle from his rounds, which were carried out every day of the week, except two, one for the rest ordained by the faith and one for him to follow his studies further. In the bleak months, he would still weave his floral cones from evergreen leaves, sprigs of scarlet berries, chains of fallen ash keys, and the funereal umbrellas of the hellebore. His rounds were harder then, though: women were more reluctant to open their doors to the gusts of chillness and the wind that swept across the plain seemed to find its purpose by sporting among Uncle Vasta's old grey suit. Often he would return with few sales achieved, and his bones as cold as Mordecai's, as he put it: the name of a friend of his youth, one of the few who had shared his studies, but had been in his tomb for many lost and now un-numbered years. Sometimes my uncle, despairing of conversation with us, would go and talk to his late friend in the graveyard about his work.

The exact object of his studies was for a long time obscure. When my mother was alive, she hovered between scorn and respect about them. But our Cousin Tamara, who was our matriarch now, was much more studiedly silent on the matter. Between us, we three who were the survivors of our family and had been arranged together by the white hands of fate, just about managed to make or find enough to keep us in meals and fuel and, at times, for each a little of our particular indulgence. For Uncle Vasta, the books, paper and ink for his studies; Cousin Tamara, the monthly musical concerts and sometimes a new hat—and as for myself? As for myself, the boy Casimir, I was content if I could get with a few pennies a scoop of warmed sunflower seeds, four mouthfuls, or if in our game of Hannibal, I rode my "elephant", a bigger boy on whose shoulders I sat astride, to victory over the others by charging, pushing, and unseating them all. Even if I was in turn cast down by the grappling hands of a rival, I and my charger would lay sprawled and laughing on the tough grass just at the very thrust and impetus of the sport, which was our game, our invention, none that the masters had devised with their solemn codes. The days when the baked seeds would fill all my senses with greedy pleasure, or our simple play gave me all I needed of ambition and consolation seemed as if they should be endless. Yet already another wisdom was waiting for me.

Sometimes I would accompany my uncle in his early morning forays into the untenanted, untended gardens where he found the freely growing flowers for his nosegays. His knowledge of these derelict places was profound. No-one I think could have known all the back streets, the hidden squares, the shunned yards, better than he, not even the imperial postman, because my uncle called at the shells of houses where no letters were ever sent. Quite why it was that certain patches of land had been given up all together by the inhabitants of our little city I do not know, and if my uncle knew, he did not say. But, aside from certain lean and shadowy cats and a drunk or two, these plots had no tenants now, and usually only us for visitors.

We would take the serpentine ways my uncle knew until we might arrive at a little sagging wooden wicket gate. Clumps of weeds clutched at it as we pushed it open, as if they wanted to push us back. The wet grasses dampened our legs with their cold tongues and the overgrown path deadened our footsteps. The glossy scales of laurel trees glimmered at us. We would stumble over half-buried rubble: worn bricks, brown medicine-bottles, the yellowing indecipherable pages of the gazette, broken spectacles, a grey felt slipper, sordid striped rags of discarded clothing, greasy and encrusted. On these middens sometimes poppies grew, raising their defiant red gonfalons over so much human detritus. And in one corner, an asteret of wild flowers might mysteriously and wondrously be strewn, whose names my uncle would murmur to himself as he gathered them: campion, feverfew, bugloss, pennyroyal, buryall.

It was on one of these dawn expeditions, with the river mist still causing pale wraiths to wander the streets, that my uncle first hinted to me about where his studies were leading. There was a green tint in the sky, as if a veil of verdigris had grown over the sun. This dimmed light seemed to reach into the stones of the houses so that they glowed with the hue of decay, and even the windows wore a veneer of brittle green. The white tendrils from the river, too, were tinged with verjuice. Regarding the horizon for a while as we stopped by the Old Bridge, my uncle sighed deeply, and it was as if his grey suit was giving up some of the icy airs of the plains it had collected during winter. He gestured at the green dawn. The sun, said my uncle, was the sole source of light from the heavens, and even the moon only gave out its reflection, while as for starlight, except to the poets, well it never reached here in any scale one could see. But sometimes, he said, it seemed to him that there was another source of light abroad in the world that did not come from the sun, but so far as he could tell emanated from certain forms already inherent in the earth before the sun had ever burst. He believed he was not the only one to have noticed this but not everyone spoke about it, and he was only telling me now, he went on, in case one day he should follow his friend Mordecai, and all his thoughts on this matter would be lost.

That day a fellow called Tomas had promised me to exchange a marble I particularly wanted for some cigarette cards of military heroes that I had secured only by valiant pestering of strangers smoking in the cafés, and so my attention to what my uncle said was not as strong as it ought to have been. But I was so far curious about his idea as to ask him what things it was that had this other light. However, here my uncle became preoccupied himself in gathering the wild flowers for the day, and said just that of course it was to be found only in those things that had always been.

I met Tomas, a long gangling lad with a thrust of yellow hair and a pockmarked face, by the gates of the Aleksander Park as we had arranged, and here we enacted our transaction. I handed him my coloured tokens, over twenty of them, each with their portrait of men wearing black and scarlet and gold, heavily whiskered and with gleaming eyes, but at the last moment Tomas insisted that there was a further part of the trade that must happen before he would surrender the marble. He held onto the hand that had given him the cards and, with a swift gesture, stabbed my forefinger with a brass pin. Then he pulled the finger towards his mouth and sucked at the seepage of blood upon his coarse tongue, before releasing his hold. I stepped back in disgust. Tomas spat into the ground and slowly brought out the treasure from his fusty pocket, wrapped in a grey rag that might once have been a handkerchief. There was a quick glint, and at last the marble was upon my palm. It was a real marble, not a glass toy: a globe of streaked colours whose peculiar hues I

particularly wanted. My fingertip stung, but I did not want
to moisten it to assuage the pain because it still bore Tomas's
spit, so I rubbed it against my thumb. We turned away from
each other and did not say another word.

At home at our table, over a mulch of swede stew with
black bread, I brought out the marble to show my uncle, and
explained how I had bargained for it. He took it between his
brown fingers and turned it over thoughtfully. Its crimson
streaks swirling through the round silver-grey ground glinted
softly in the lamp-light. He handed it back to me and said,
with a gentle lightness, that it was quite possible this was one
of the old things that held the original light, and so I was
right to have exchanged it for the garish cards celebrating
famous murderers, no matter how many gilt decorations
they had around their collars. He could see, he went on, that
I had understood the importance of preserving the ancient
and beautiful, and that made him wonder if after all our
family might not have that as a particular trust, deep in our
blood. Even you, Tamara, he said, with your love of amber
hat pins, reverence the older light. I cannot say if he was
simply being kind, and wanted to admire my new toy and
add some romance to it, or if he really did think this way:
but what he said sounded a golden clarion in my sharp ears.

Cousin Tamara's safeguard against all that our existence
sent us was silence. It was neither a sullen nor a resigned
silence, but simply the outward expression, as I see now, of
a great reserve of resilience. I sometimes wondered if she was
simply keeping in her mind the music that was her solace
and joy. She wore her stone-coloured hair in braids of tight
round knots, like clefs' heads, as if the music wanted to
burst out from her head. After my Uncle Vasta had talked a
little more about the ancient light and the idea that perhaps
families of a certain lineage might exist to serve it, she quietly
gathered up the supper dishes and beckoned me to help her

with them. It was her way of removing me, without making a big fuss about it, from his peculiar speculations.

But naturally I was filled with pride at the idea that my uncle had advanced. I did not pause to doubt it, but adopted it at once as most certainly true. Like many children, I secretly felt that I was different and apart from everyone else, that my thoughts and feelings were rare and unusual. And what my uncle had thought aloud answered to those urgings within me. I began to regard my schoolfellows with a sense of distance, as if what they did had no importance to me: it was all very well, and must be tolerated, but it was not what was real. I expected at any moment that some grand figure would stop me in the street and summon me away, or be introduced into our classroom and beckon only to me, and I would be told quite definitely about my mysterious destiny to serve the older light. Over and over in my mind I rehearsed the scene and how I, delicately aware of how to balance a look both haughty and humble, would say farewell to my classmates and follow the great stranger to my higher training.

I began to seek in the books that I read for signs of the special things that must hold the light older than the sun, and found clues in many places. Surely Aladdin's lamp must be one of these, and shining it up drew the old light out: the genie, I could see, was a way of saying that this light had a strange and different life. The roc's egg that Sinbad sought must also be one of the great and ancient things. When I read stories of magic cups, I knew that they must be formed of the same high dust. I even thought that Rapunzel's hair must have caught some speck of this original sorcery within it, and very likely, I reasoned, Cousin Tamara might have done so too, which was why she kept her hair so tightly knotted, to keep the secret.

What perplexed me was how I must spend my time while I waited for the call to take up the mission of my lineage. And I was also worried that my mind might be stained by the unclean things I had to see as I walked around our town. They would grow in my mind so that I could only see them and not the shining things that ought to be my quest. A dog slobbering with a rat in its mouth; an ex-soldier with a yellow face; a tree weeping green slime; the dirty ruts and dank puddles of the road; swollen women waiting in queues; all these seemed to taint my imagination. So I came to shun the more crowded ways and take myself to the lonelier edges, where I could train my gaze only on the wild and pure. Still, it was hard sometimes to stop my thoughts wandering towards the coarse, grotesque things: and I wondered if my failure here was stopping the herald I expected from coming to me, to announce my new destiny.

It did not take me long to reason that the sordid things of the earth were enemies and assailants, laying siege to the crystal truth I held within. But how was I to defend myself? This dilemma seized me like a cruel ecstasy until I knew that I must share it with someone. I would sometimes start to talk to my uncle about it, but found that he would hurriedly, and in a muddled way, try to retract what he had said before about our family's allegiance to the old original light. I expect Tamara had spoken to him about it. Do not take me too seriously, Casimir, he would murmur, I am just a dreamer. But later, crouched in his woven shawl over a clutter of papers, my uncle spoke to me quietly, in a voice hardly distinguishable from the fluttering of the oil lamp, about the matter that troubled him most. He was by now quite convinced upon this question of the other light, he said, that was not in dispute. But what worried him was whether this light was lawful, whether its origin could be condoned, or whether even by noticing it he might have become complicit in some matter that it was wrong for him to know.

So far from deflecting me, these speculations naturally excited me further. Not only was I the secret rightful guardian of a great thing, but also of a forbidden thing. And certainly that explained why the messenger was slow to make himself known. This must be done clandestinely, at some fortuitous hour. I stayed awake some nights in case darkness was necessary for the visitor's arrival, my skin all raised with feverish expectation, as if my whole body was an abrasion. Some dim light trickled in through the shutters and illuminated the dusky cornices and cracked walls with a sort of grey steely glow. I wondered if this could be a sign that the figure sent to fetch me was not far off, that he might soon be made manifest.

Both my uncle and my cousin soon discerned that I was keeping some secret to myself, and each tried in their ways to turn me towards new interests. We had no money for a doctor or even as a gift-offering to a scholar who might cajole me out of my little youthful heresy, so I was spared their attentions. But Uncle Vasta explained to me that even if he was right about the old forgotten source of light, there was no one else who thought that way anymore, so I should not think too much about it. He had only meant to compliment me on the choice of the scarlet-adorned marble, to show his pleasure at my good taste. But I could hear that he did not say these words from the heart: and besides, he did not stop his studies of the subject, and even began to bring into the house stones and pebbles that he thought had some faint aura of light about them, which could be residual evidence of his theory.

Cousin Tamara was more practical with me. She gave me tasks to do in the town so that I might not wander out into the waste land at its edge so often, and she gave me, from her small earnings as a seamstress, presents she thought might catch and divert my interests. Out of an embarrassed boyish sense of courtesy, I gave these some attention at first, but soon put them by. Patiently, however, she tried new things, until one day, whether by careful thought or chance, she found a more than temporary distraction for me. It was a big atlas, out of date and well-used, its pages only just clinging to a delicate mesh in the binding, as if the book had been put together by an unusually learned spider.

My cousin turned the pages with me to show me the lands where Aladdin, Sinbad, Parzifal and Rapunzel lived, and I soon came to see the atlas as a wonderfully-hued storehouse of stories. The colours and contours of the countries and their mountains, rivers and coasts, did not represent to me physical or political features, but the lineaments of legend. We had been taken by rote through some ink-blotted, black-lettered monochrome maps at school, but this vast atlas was as different to those as my imagined world of those who served the original light was to the "real" dullness I found every day. And of course I wanted to know what golden myths were told of the other places marked on the map, whose very pages had a thick gloss that seemed to be the outward promise of the shining things it held within.

To my cousin, this must have seemed a more innocent and educational preoccupation than the one my uncle had prompted in me, and I was allowed to spend many hours simply studying the atlas. But in truth this new interest was not different in kind from my dreams of a finer world governed by a stranger light. It was just that I had changed my thinking about how this might happen. Instead of waiting for some gilded herald to come to me, I saw that I must go out, at first in my daydreams, but one day in very reality, to the great and curious regions printed on the vast pages of the map book. I soon built up my own itinerary of potent places, whose names called out to me. Some essence in the ordering of the letters of these names, often sharp and strange, odd and outlandish, spoke to my own private delight: probably no other child would have chosen exactly the same particular syllables; but these were mine.

And that is why Cartagena, Latakia, Curaçao, Batum, Trevancore, Tokelau, Yunnanfu, and Zutphen became the companions of my youth. Companions indeed, for I came to regard them not as places but as characters, as forms. I would open the heavy pages of the atlas, and turn to where each of them were shown, greeting them like a friend and letting their particular quality steal into my mind. They were angels, princes and godlings: Curaçao with a shining blue helmet and winged feet; Batum with a green turban, robes and draggling whiskers; Tokelau a tall brown youth with amber eyes. All of them, of course, were adherents of the older light, like me: and one day, I was sure, we would meet. In the meantime, their spirits accompanied me in my mind as I stalked the streets of our town.

I saw less of my Uncle Vasta, but I knew that he went out at night, no longer looking for wild flowers, but seeking instead for the niches and facets of the original light, that might be found glimmering in the darkness. His flesh became greyer, closer to the worn sheen of his old suit: he would say to us that soon he would have more time to talk to Mordecai. The predictions and maxims upon the little scrolls of yellow paper became curter and more enigmatic: some that had escaped his sorting and lay like sleeping, never-transformed caterpillars upon the floor, would be found to bear no letters that Cousin Tamara or I could identify. At this, even my silent cousin would sigh, and look at me closely, as if asking herself whether I would soon start writing undecipherable prophecies too.

Uncle Vasta, when he was turning over in his mind once more whether the older light were lawful or not, made me promise (perhaps at our cousin's urging, perhaps from his own conscience) that I would not do as he did, and go looking for those things that held it still. You have a different future, boy, he urged me, putting as much fierce insistence into his brittle eyes as he would summon up from his paled form. And to this reluctant oath I was faithful. Whether with or without my companions, the gods of the cities and islands of the atlas, I did not roam our town looking for the glowing stones, for the glass that glinted where there was no sun, for the bronze in old coins that held its own sheen, for the books whose yellow paper, hidden from the day, yet still possessed a secret bloom.

Yet I could hardly help it if sometimes, when I least expected it, munching a handful of the silver seeds, or hailing again a comrade of the days of Hannibal, I would still sometimes see, from the corner of my eye, some delicate hint of the original light, emitting its faint and ancient radiance like a gentle signal.

The Unrest at Aachen

All that storm has passed, and still the Moselle flows: and from my study I can see the great green hands of the fig trees guarding their secret fruit with its frail bloom, and the purple bruise of its flesh. And I can see the autumn sun glint on the tilted panes of the summer house, sparking silver lances of light. Here, I hope to reach the age of my old mentor, that great statesman, and to occupy my time as fruitfully as the vines of the valley by writing down what I can reveal of my career, starting with that strange affair of the casket of Charlemagne—and the return of the paladins.

By the time I allow this to be read, there will be no harm (whatever has become of us) in revealing that the Luxembourg secret service came into being soon after the accession of Grand Duke William in 1905. He foresaw that our independence relied upon understanding the intentions and attitudes of our more powerful neighbours. We had only gained full autonomy in 1890 when the Dutch king, who was also our archduke, died. The Dutch throne passed to his daughter, but our duchy did not. It continued in the next nearest male line. So we were then fully separated from the Netherlands, and become our own state. And that is how we want it to be. We have a motto: *Mir wölle bleiwe, war mir sin.* What we have, we hold, as you might say.

But in early 1906 this was now precarious. Our ruler himself had no male heirs, and intended to change the constitution to allow his daughters to succeed. This might call into question the entire basis of our sovereignty. He needed to understand how the powers would regard this—might Prussia in particular, as it had over Schleswig-Holstein, insist on the Salic law, and exploit the position to seize and occupy our Grand Duchy, which it had coveted for much of the last century? It was clear we needed to hinder Prussia's ambitions, and know what England and France might do. There were four of us in the new service, Michael Esper, Stephanie Voorn, Willie Ulff and myself, Yann Medermain, stationed mainly in Berlin, Paris, London and on our borders respectively.

I was given the borders post as the youngest, since of course it was the nearest to home, where I might seek advice if needed (and—no doubt—be easily recalled too). I made my base in Aachen, where our Grand Dukes had three times been crowned as Holy Roman Emperors, in Charlemagne's cathedral, on his marble throne. From here I could easily visit Liège, Maastricht, Cologne, Lorraine, to sense the temper of the times and discreetly elicit information.

We reported only to President-of-the-Council Paul Eyschen, with his distinguished white hair fiercely combed back from a long brow, and his splendid white beard and moustaches. He combined his role with that of Foreign Minister, as was our custom. He had once been our representative to the German Empire and knew quite well their ways. I have heard it said that M. Eyschen was over-dignified and distant. Certainly, he was determined to secure for our small country the respect it was rightfully due, and so protocol was important to him. Yet he had entered the chamber very young, strictly before the required age of twenty-five, and despite his more than sixty years now, he still had a cordiality for the youthful. This is why, I think, he agreed to my appointment: he perhaps saw himself in my eager twenty-five years.

"M. Medermain," he said, "solid people will say things to a foolish young man that they would not say to a graver or more worldly man. So use your foolishness of youth well. Let them be glad to explain things to you. Listen, and mark what you hear: but do not appear to do so. *Au revoir*."

We four wrote to each other in our own tongue, which might have been code enough, since no other nation speaks it. But we did not trust to this—there might very well be some German Herr Professor with a gold pince-nez who had studied it as a "dialect"—and so we encoded our correspondence too. I confess that to a keen young man this was both romantic and yet tiresome, since in my attic room, looking out over the Aachen steeples and the stone galleons of its public buildings, I had to slowly work through the cipher, when I had rather be wandering the violet dusk of its tree-lined streets and squares.

But I persevered, and I remember well how Willie wrote to us from London, with his typical gusto. "One of their leading novelists, Mr. William Le Queux, has written a book all about a German invasion of Britain in a few years time. It is being serialised. Everyone is talking about it and eagerly they read each new episode as it comes out. Ministers have had to respond to questions about the navy and the shore defences. It seems to me the English would go to war with our big neighbour now over anything. Even for us! More books are following as other writers leap upon the farm cart. In their public houses, and even in the Lyons tea houses, I hear nothing but vehemence."

I could imagine Willy, who was quite a gourmand, forcing himself to drink their brown beer, the colour (so he complained) of gutter-mud, or sip their thin tea, also (so he explained) the colour of gutter-mud, though in this case mixed with grey rainwater, so that he could eavesdrop on all these fierce discussions of the English. I was glad my own role called for acquaintances of a higher standing.

From Paris, Stephanie Voorn shared a subtler insight: "The Second Empire is the current mode here. All the gilded chairs, allegorical oils, swags, cartouches, waxed moustaches, elaborate bonnets, stuffed satin, acidic yellow and midnight purple of that era are back in vogue. You do not wish for fashion talk? Consider this: a nation that fondly remembers its last empire is preparing for another, or so I believe. The lost war with Prussia is unfinished business. Soon, the seconds will be summoned, and the duel commence. And the affront requiring satisfaction? Any cause might do. It might even be the old boundaries again."

And as for me, I wrote to them of Aachen (as if indeed they had never heard of it!—ah, the knowledge of youth!)—"it is a liminal town in the furthest west of Germany, an ancient, fallen city, and its thermal springs and the great cathedral with the shrine of Charlemagne bring many visitors. So, it is a place of strangers and pilgrims. But even the inhabitants do not feel a part of the Empire. 'It is a long way from Berlin,' one fellow remarked to me, 'and we are nearer our neighbours.' Like us, they speak and mingle French and German quite equally (they do not have the advantage of our Luxembourgish) and I believe the educated prefer French, and recall quite fondly the days when they were Aix-le-Chapelle. 'Let us be frank,' one great lady said to me, 'that name even sounds so much finer, does it not? *Aix-le-Chapelle*'—this fell from her lips like a gentle zephyr—'or Aachen?'—this she made sound like an impediment in the throat or a dog growling in its sleep. It is my conclusion from such intimations that the people here would frown upon any Prussian adventuring in our country: they would see us almost as cousins. They would not willingly condone an occupation: but I do not think they could be relied upon to come to our aid unless very provoked. The garrison here is mostly local Rhenish-men, with some Westphalians too; but some of the officers are East Prussians. They would have to be removed."

The relish with which I wrote that last phrase, as if it might be my task, for the sake of the Grand Duchy, to "remove" the lean and scarred-faced jaegers. From my mentor back in the capital of our Grand Duchy, came terse advice: "See what can be done to assist the provocation." The great lady I quoted had been the Margravina Augusta. I had been furnished with an introduction to her by friends in Luxembourg, and because of my callow years she consented to walk out with me, as she wielded her jade-green parasol with its carved and painted parrot's head, promenading the Elisenbrunnen. In those ornamental gardens, where the long, elegant shadows of the colonnade played upon the lawns, and the flower beds displayed a Gallic population of dandyish or demure creatures in many bright hues, within Teutonic borders, neatly box-hedged and demarcated by iron hoops, she made clear her sympathies. Supposedly she was in the city for her health, but really I think because her relations found her too formidable to keep at home, and encouraged the polite fiction that she must convalesce. She explained to me the notables of the city, pointing the ferrule of her verdant sunshade at people of interest who were either "very *Aix*, you know" or "much too *Aachen*". Everyone in the city, it seemed, invalid or inhabitant, came to the gardens at least once in the day to enjoy their calm—or perhaps the parading of society. When she discovered my interest as a student in the history of the old city (for that was my ostensible reason for being there—my "cover"), she insisted on introducing me to a young protégé, whom she said knew it better than any.

This young man, about my own age, was an ardent student of the *Chansons de Geste*, and knew all the names of the paladins of Charlemagne by heart, and (I am sure) those of their chargers too. His was a mind thoroughly medieval and he spoke of these paragons of chivalry almost as if they were his daily companions. The horn of Roland, the spells of the enchanter Maugris, the gleaming silver shield of loyal Oliver, the brave pennon (like a dragon's long scarlet tongue) of fair Ivon, all were as though vividly real to him, and in me he found a willing listener. Guy Zaina had also first come to the city as a convalescent and the marks of his illness still showed in the spectral lean-ness of his form, the white face and lank golden hair and the dark eye-sockets, so that he was like some frail tall pale flower. What gave him the will to exist was his burning passion for those romances that had grown around the Emperor Charlemagne, and his retinue, whose echoes might linger still in all the city's high stone chambers, hidden hallowed churches, and the houses of the guilds, with their carven blazonry.

I wandered with him the avenues, byways and courtyards of the old city, all among its stones the colour of worn amber or carnelian, under the steep pitch of its slate roofs, and the watch of its high, diamond-paned windows. Here, he reminded me, thirty kings had in their days been crowned, the Holy Roman Emperors had in ancient times been anointed, great nobles and knights, learned prelates, had all known its holy ground. "It is the very crown of Europe," he would exclaim. And if its state was a little fallen now, if it had become a backwater for invalids and idle sightseers, this only increased the golden allure of its former days. He took me late one afternoon in the gilded air of a slow dusk to the great portal of the cathedral, and we strode solemnly, as if in a liturgy, towards the *Karlsschrein*, the high shrine of Charlemagne, with its carved and gleaming panels, and its figures and reliefs illuminated by exquisite enamels, and embellished by deep-hued gems: a masterpiece of the medieval goldsmiths from the Rhine and Meuse country. It was a silent, haughty symbol of the civilisation of these Western lands from an epoch when the East, now so dominant, was a swamp infested by pagans, outlaws, savages. To my surprise, my friend knelt and murmured a prayer there, as I stood awkwardly by: and it was as if for a moment the golden light from the sacred casket cast a bloom upon his face, a rare radiance that annealed his pale flesh with a glow of benediction.

It was indeed this noble history that led to the first hint of the potential for that *provocation* that my mentor had told me to look out for. Our agent in Berlin, Michael, was the last of us to file a report, partly because (we learnt) he thought that the German police were suspicious of him, so he had needed to proceed with care. But his conclusions were thoughtful and unusual. "All who speak of the ambitions of Germany assert that it is its military who wield most power in the land. It is true they are strong and ambitious, but I believe they are also cautious. No: the danger comes, I believe, from another source; from its professors. The Emperor holds audience with these doctors of law, of history, of divinity, of philosophy and they flatter his intellect. He is quite convinced by them that he is the true heir of a vast and terrible destiny: the mastery of Europe. With many persuasions from old chronicles and canons they convince him of this. And he listens, without a doubt he listens. Beware, then, Paris and London, for here is a new Napoleon; beware even little Aix, my Yann, for here even is Charlemagne reborn."

Soon after, in the salons, soirées, promenades, parties and receptions that diverted the city's gentility through all the ennui of recuperation or rustication, I began to hear shards of conversation accompanied by much waggling of heads and fluttering of fingers. As I passed among these cognoscenti, the men with their imperials and medals, the ladies with their silk gowns and arch fans, I would catch hold of such terse, thrilled, shocked remarks as these:

" . . . to have it opened."

"Opened? Not—the casket?"

"At the request of the Most Highest."

"To what end?"

"For purposes of *historical research*."

"But surely: the Church?"

"Opposed, but bending."

"The City?"

"Obsequious."

"Then only . . . "

"Quite."

Berlin, it appeared, had requested —ordered—the unsealing of the golden shrine, that seven hundred year old treasure erected by Frederick II to house Charlemagne's sacred remains. The mayor and the bishop had acquiesced, were given little choice. They issued measured explanations. This matter would be carried out and completed at night, and would not disturb the cathedral's liturgical round. Master craftsmen would be sent to undertake the task, and no damage would be done to the gilded ark. The clergy and the city elders had solemnly considered the request and were satisfied, and they would be represented at the unsealing. The relics of great and holy men had often been examined before: it was not unusual or disrespectful

Yet, as ever happens with startling news, all these soothing nuances were at once lost to view and the folk of Aachen knew one thing only: the men of the capital were going to break into their emperor's tomb. And speculation rose up at once about the one thing that had been left unsaid. Why? For it was indeed the Most High himself who had commanded this, and royalty does not give reasons, its purpose is inscrutable. Rumours darted like martins across the roofs of the city. Perhaps he is testing our loyalty, our compliance with his wishes: or simply wishes to assert his dominion here. Or, others said, *ah*, the Kaiser wants the bones of the true Emperor in Berlin. They are to be removed under pretext of scholarship, but really so that he can gloat over the relics.

It is perfectly clear to us why he wants them: he must see himself as the new imperial ruler of Europe, perhaps even as the Holy Roman Emperor. He who has the relics, has the reign, so he might suppose. They say even that he consults astrologers on the matter: whether the time is right to unleash his legions across the continent, with Charlemagne's bones at their spearhead.

And the whispers began to travel on the wind. Willy heard them even over the sea: "The rumours are reaching here. The English have begun to see the Grail again, in defiance I have no doubt." From Paris, Stephanie wrote: "The French are reciting the 'Song of Roland' and remembering their old *romans*. Charlemagne is *their* king, they say. Look out." In Berlin, a harder-pressed Michael: "The professors are quacking to the Court about the obtuseness of those outlanders in the West."

I ensured that the story also reached Aachen's sister city of Trèves (or Trier, as the Germans had it), to the south, with hints that its ancient cathedral's most sacred relic, the Holy Tunic, might be next on the Kaiser's list. Soon there were reports of concern in high places there, and the eminents of the cities consulted one another, and then reached out to their neighbours. A League of the West was discussed, a spiritual confederation of the marchlands, to celebrate and preserve these time-honoured realms from the depredations of the upstart capital in the East. This, too, was part of my design, for I saw that we could help to build a buffer of disaffection between central Prussia and our own Grand Duchy.

Soon the story of the assault on Aix's most sacred shrine was beyond the ability of the city council to control, no matter what firm assertions or placatory explanations it might issue. This hitherto calm, even sleepy, border city was exercised by a wild ferment made up of indignation, excitement, and a proud memory of its past as an Imperial Free City—a city, that is, of the Holy Roman, not the medieval German, Empire. With sly words, an innocent question, an apparent baffled doubt about all the fuss, the subtle twisting of a poker in the hearth-fire to make the flames leap higher, I played my assiduous part in provoking this further, as did my allies, the pro-French Margravina and the young romancer Guy Zaina.

And then—an omen. Jackdaws had nested for centuries in the interstices of the octagon tower of the cathedral, in the crockets and greaves of its aerial filigree. Some fissure in the fabric, some over-inquisitiveness, had led them to fall in to the great domed chapel itself and wheel within the sacred air, dazzled by the bright regalia and swooping upon it as if to peck out gemstones, glittering enamel, gilt and silverwork. It was only with great difficulty that they were ushered out through the great door, discoursing loudly.

The Mayor made a special statement. The medieval chest is to be inspected by learned gentlemen, professors, doctors, from the universities. They wish to examine only the ancient cloth in which the relics are wrapped, to see if it might be replicated for a museum or gallery. If it can be, the city itself might house such a marvellous re-creation for a while. It is not enough. He is scarcely believed. Even those who listen to the story give it a new cast. So, it is the emperor's own shroud they would take is it? Or, so they would weave a cloak for the Kaiser from the silk that Charlemagne wore? Is that to be it? Discontent rises. Then lights are seen in the Cathedral late at night, and it is said strangers were glimpsed being ushered through a quiet side-door. Black-coated men with sinister despatch cases were noted departing from the railway station on a train to the East, taking private compartments.

A grand procession formed on the night following the culmination of these rumours, and the accusation, neither confirmed nor denied by the authorities, that the emissaries from Berlin had completed their sacrilegious work in secrecy and left, as a "thief in the night". Suppose a city possessed of spirits sleeping in its stones, in the arches, lintels, pillars, steps, slabs, pediments of its very fabric: and suppose that once in a while on certain occasions these are released to be free of its streets once again: that was how the procession seemed. I took up a vantage point to watch it pass. No quarter, no level, no element of the old city was omitted from this solemn parade. We had done our work well.

First, there was the silent reproachful vanguard of white-cowled divines, defying their superiors, and bearing flaming torches which made the shadows race and writhe, or flailing silver censers whose gleams sent stars of light into the night, and whose cedarwood fumes stirred the mind to thoughts of sanctity and deep ancient power. They were followed by the guildsmen, with their tabards of gold and scarlet, their plumed caps, and their ceremonial spurs, with the staunchest carrying banners and oriflammes bearing devices of heraldic beasts—lions, wyverns, eagles, dragons—which seemed to quicken in the silken shimmering, as if they might at once pounce out upon those who threatened ancient liberties.

Many serried ranks of the respectable followed, in their garb of black and silver, bearing medals, ribbons, chains of office, and other insignia, pacing ponderously as if they were part of the obsequies of an eminent citizen. Veterans, merchants, officials, professionals, the formidable gentlewomen of the town in their most dignified gowns, strode purposefully by.

They were followed by the "mechanick" trades in their blue drill, with sturdy, set faces, and then in bright contrast the actors, designers and stage-hands of the Imperial Theatre, who had raided the wardrobe as if for a pageant, and appeared in medieval costume as knights, squires, pages, great ladies, monks and soldiers of an era which might pass for that of Charlemagne, at least in the romances. Following them, rejoicing in all this vivid recreation of the chronicles he so loved, was my friend Zaina, reciting at intervals choice passages from the lays and verses of the romances, and invoking the champions of Charlemagne's mythical court.

After these, the under-classes of the city attached themselves to the tail of the procession, in a laughing, jeering, jostling throng; the street women, beggars, itinerant musicians, boy arabs, drunkards, derelicts, opium incurables. From somewhere in this throng, there burst through a fat comedian wearing a spiked helmet and absurd twirling false moustaches, tripping over a ludicrously large sword, and swathed only in a huge sheet edged with splashed purple, which might be taken to represent the stolen (as it was supposed) shroud of the ancient High Emperor.

This proved too much for the sub-commander of the militia, who had been forced to gnaw his anger as this "treasonous" procession passed. Such a stark snub, such a satire on the Most High whom he was sworn to serve could not be countenanced. With a cry he urged his dark-caparisoned steed forward, and made as if to crack the oafish comedian with the flat of his sword. But naturally his men, a small detachment of a dozen or so reserve cavalry, followed as if by instinct his abrupt surge forward, and were not so discriminating in the wielding of their weapons. The pranks and cavortings of the disreputable rump of the parade changed at once to mad flight, squeals, oaths and shouts of protest, and before the melee could be undone, the impromptu cavalry charge had driven straight into the back of the procession from the theatre. Soon the street looked like the gaudy aftermath of some fierce tournament.

At the first lunge of the military, I had myself impetuously rushed forward from my vantage point, to bear witness to what was to follow. And as the horses were wheeled abruptly away, and the confusion began to clear, I heard from beneath a lamp, a hoarse cry—*Carolus Magnus! Carolus Magnus!* I recognised the impassioned voice and cast about wildly for its source, until I saw young Guy Zaina slumped against the ornate column of a street-light, his volume of romances limply held in his pale fingers, and repeating simply the stark, proud epitaph of the great king. I rushed to his side. All of one pale temple had been crushed and a dark purple bruise was forming there, from which there was a staunchless scarlet ebbing . I called out for help, for a doctor, but already I could see it was too late. Zaina raised his eyes to the skies and they seemed to dim for a few flickering seconds, then blaze up again: "The paladins have come!" he proclaimed, "Oliver, Ivon, Engelier, Ivoire, Anséis, Girard—they are here, they are here!"

I looked around involuntarily as if it might really be so. I saw the rag-taggle residue of the mummers in their medieval dress and their cardboard armour, their silver paint, their property swords and blunt, broken lances.

"Yes, they are here," I assured him. He nodded with an infinitely slow, gentle movement of his head and forced his lips into a fixed smile. A final smile.

I stood up. The last of the theatrical troupe had scuttled away, except perhaps one: by the shadow of a porphyry column there was a tall figure, like a detachment of darkness. It seemed to me there were movements all about it, like the floating of a cloak, or the flying of a banner, or the flourishing of a sword. Could it have been simply the flickerings from the debris strewn all about in the aftermath of the charge? My sight was subdued, blurred, and I could not be sure of what I could see.

But I could be sure of what I ought to see. Within hours, the vision of the young romancer was sweeping like a wild roaring wind through the streets and the very stones of the city. The paladins had been seen! The return, the return! They had come at the fervent prayer of a gallant young martyr. Soon, it transpired, others had certainly seen them too, at the watch-towers of the city walls, at the great door of the cathedral, even in the white stars and the slow purple sunset. For some days afterwards they were still seen, as many would testify, perhaps with all sincerity, and they drew to them any mysterious echo or shadow or glint of light or uncanny sound that the city could furnish, of which, in the natural course of things, there will always be an abundance. The *return of the paladins* was now a fact to which other facts could be attracted, a myth patient for embellishment. Yet I confess my heart was no longer in the work.

There was no further attempt to inspect the relics of Charlemagne. A cavalry commander was reprimanded and moved, later promoted. A chill note from the French Ambassador asking for assurances as to the safety of his country's citizens in *Aix-le-Chapelle* was briskly acknowledged.

Perhaps these activities in Aachen, and the reports of our agents abroad, prevented an outburst of war in Europe in 1906, despite how bellicose the nations were. The German potentate was taken aback by the resistance to his designs for the relics of the illustrious Emperor of the Romans, and saw because of this that he could not now rely even upon the cities within his existing borders. So while he sulked, our Grand Duke was able to proceed with his plans to change the laws of succession in Luxembourg, so that we should always have an heir and always be independent. There was scarcely a signal of protest: we had achieved a *fait accompli*. Our mission was a success. Yet, it is true we had only achieved a temporary respite: it would not be long before we were called upon to thwart further designs upon our country.

And whatever I saw by the column at Aachen, I trust that, in the land of legends, Guy Zaina will always ride under the banner of the paladins, his white face gilded by the glamour of Charlemagne.

The Mascarons
of the Late Empire

It was the dream of Dr. Julius Barusch to found the world's first New Latinist city, a place where all who spoke the proposed pan-European language could gather to use it as an everyday tongue, in the streets, in the markets, in business and in the cafés and taverns. As soon as the world saw, thought Dr. Barusch, the way it worked so freely and simply among men and women of every nationality and none, of every allegiance and creed, then the impetus for the fullest possible adoption of New Latin would become unstoppable.

Furthermore, as he knew from his own many friendships, and his correspondence, those who practised New Latin were often people of the broadest sympathies and modern outlook, who might be expected to be amongst the vanguard of those rebuilding European civilisation from the rubble of the Great War. The adoption of this new, neutral tongue based on a common classical heritage could only help foster international amity. Dr. Barusch often thought and spoke like that, in resonant phrases, and they would excite his corpulent frame with a strange, almost fleshly thrill. For it was not only his ideals that were globular; so was his form, despite the efforts of his silver-grey waistcoats to contain him, as if it too wanted to absorb all it could of the world in a vast embrace.

It had taken Dr. Barusch some time to alight upon the city suitable for his campaign, but that city was now firmly fixed in his plans, and he had taken up residence there. Two prongs were part of that plan; to convert the existing population, at least starting with the most educated part of it, to New Latin; and to attract its speakers from across the world to join him there and help spread the word. The city he had chosen was: ah, now there was the point; it had at least four different names according to which of its many minorities (there was no majority) one asked.

It did not daunt Dr. Barusch in the least that the city already had at least these four languages in common use, and its own *patois* drawn indiscriminately from the most pungent and forceful extremities of all of them; nor that it had several lesser-known tongues in local use; nor that it also had an official, as it were diplomatic, language that was none of these others. All the stronger the case, he maintained, to encourage the use of a single, simple, unaffiliated tongue, and to welcome others to come and speak it.

The variegation of the city was not only to be discerned in its daily Babel: for it also had the holy buildings of at least five faiths, and some said six or seven, depending what you counted. At almost any ascent of one of the cobbled slopes coming up from the muddy river, or at most turns of the little tunnel-like alleyways that wriggled through the city like wormholes, or from within the serenity of the beech or birch groves of its public gardens, there would rise a tower, a dome, a cluster of cupolas, a jagged row of crenellations, a spire, or some fantastic assemblage of several of these, which, when the dust blew from the east or the faint far scent of pine resin from the wooded mountains to the west, would sometimes seem to ripple, like reflections in a dark lake. And in this city, sometimes so curiously unreal, Dr. Julius Barusch thought he could found the first society devoted to the spread and perfection of the European language, and all the humanitarian ideals it implied.

The city was not the first that Dr. Barusch had considered for the realisation of his dream. From Ancona and Aarhus to

Zürich and Zaragoza, he had explored many: but it was only here, amongst a restless, quick-witted, resilient and hybrid population, that he thought he had found fertile ground. At the Café de l'Europe he made his base, taking an accustomed place close to the window, among the cream-and-chocolate plaster flourishes of the walls, the great crimson velvet swags of the curtains, and the hefty deep oak chairs. Here he would linger long over a succession of black coffees flavoured with cardamom, served together with a few of the sugar-sprinkled biscuits known as cat's tongues (which, being beige lozenges, they resembled neither in colour nor form—a fine example of the illogicality of the old languages). He would place discreetly upon the table a little desk flag bearing the New Latin symbol, the radiant sun, as a sign that he was open for interlocution in the new tongue. Even the waiters in their long aprons would wryly join in, murmuring the New Latin names when they brought him the hot dark treacly liquid and its attendant confection, or if he asked instead for a mineral water.

Often he was joined by one of his "discoveries" in the city, M. Aurelian Zothe, who had come here from Constantinople on a Nansen passport for the stateless, as part of a quota the Norwegian diplomat had patiently negotiated with the power for the time being in charge of the city. But what Zothe's origins actually were, before he gained the ingenious, if tentative, protection of this League of Nations scheme for exiles and the dispossessed, no-one really knew, and Zothe could not, or would not, exactly say. His appearance gave few clues: his face was sharp-featured, almost triangular, and his pale blue eyes were somewhat almondine in their watchful shape. Whatever had befallen him en route to and from the Golden Horn had not reduced the tailoring of his sleekly-cut suit, nor the blaze of the ties in pomegranate and pistachio hues that he wore, nor the sheen upon his pointed shoes.

But Zothe had a trade or craft for which, just at present, there was a certain demand. With the aftermath of the war, cities and their streets were adopting different shapes and names, borders and boundaries were shifting: and all of these needed the services of a skilled and subtle mapmaker. And that was Aurelian Zothe's knack, to make order out of labyrinths and imaginary lines. It was even said of him that he had once mastered the notoriously uncharted old quarters of Venice or the writhing congeries of Naples, but he did not claim this himself. He could, however, simplify matters for the visitor or the new arrival, and illustrate his plans too with pleasing touches: fine lettering, heraldic illustrations, dashes of colour. And he had them made in all the many tongues of both the inhabitants and the visitors, so that there was something of the familiar they could grasp even as they struggled to learn the city's strange serpentine topography. So that, in this city and most of the nearest cities, it soon became known that a Zothe street map was the first thing to acquire, from one of the little wooden newspaper or tobacco kiosks.

It could not be said that Zothe was persuaded that language could be simplified as readily as he dealt with streets; and often when his ovoid and orotund friend gave forth upon his New Latinist vision, a little cynical smile could be seen to pluck at his thin lips. He privately thought that even if a language could be used to unite men, they would soon find other things to divide them: emblems and symbols, for example, seemed ever to excite those who wished to stress their difference. Stateless himself, he found it strange how a certain combination of shapes and colours could have that effect upon people. Even the New Latinists, with their brave radiant sun, were not immune from this curious fever. But for all that, his affection (and gratitude for the help Dr. Barusch had given him when he first debouched here) over-rode his doubts, and he had gone so far as to design a New Latin atlas for the time when the great scheme should come to fruition.

On this day Dr. Barusch had waddled around the folk hostels of all the different nationalities that were dotted around the perimeter of the city, leaving his New Latin leaflets for guests to pick up, and wishing (and not only for his personal convenience) there had been just one great international hostel: and he had made his way back through the hubbub of the ringing red and white trams, the bawling of the horse-cab-drivers, the rapid chattering of the sparrows, the mangled patois of the street arabs and the dramatic drum-roll of barrels being unloaded, to the swirling silver handles and gilt-painted glass of his favourite café, which he entered with a compassionate sigh for himself, and sank into the deep cushioned oak of his chair. Zothe was already there, inhaling a bitter spirit, and drawing upon a narrow black cigarette. They enjoyed a companionable silence for a few moments. Though the café was quite full, it was still a haven from the squalling of the city: here, conversations were held in murmurs, orders were served deftly with the minimum of clatter, and even the soft tap of chess pieces could be made out, from the specially cordoned alcoves for the game. In one of these, indeed, lost in his own thoughts, the two could see and nod to the regular who gazed upon an unusual circular board, whose pieces splayed out in radial lines. With a black round cap, and a shapeless gathering of cloaks and shawls, the player was unmistakeable; but he too, as with so many others, was of uncertain origin or prospect.

It was in just this contented quiet that the young scholar Michael Vay found them when he ventured through the doors of the old golden café. He was wearied by the long haul from the station on the northern edge of the city and from the slow train journey before that, through miles of marshland, dull plains, fields pockmarked with shell craters, and abandoned farms whose walls still bore the signs of flames or a tattoo of bullet holes. And perhaps his visit here might be futile. Vay was at the very end of a study he had begun when he had been a promising student, in the lost days before the war. It was left unfinished when the conflict broke out, and while he had served as an engineer on the Galician front there had seldom been the time to study the local cities with other than a military eye. But now, though he doubted it would ever be published or read, an obstinacy marked in the bone structure of his axe-shaped head, the flesh accentuated and made paler by the privations of the war, had made him persist in his treatise.

Here at last he hoped to finish this annotated catalogue of certain architectural sculptures in the great buildings of the empire, or, as was now quite certainly the case, the late empire. For the vast magic carpet world in which he had grown up, full of strange patterns and rich colours, even if frayed a little at the edges, had been diminished at the end of the war into a worn, scorched hearth-rug.

This city had once been, perhaps in theory still was, but soon might not be, once the treatifying had concluded, the furthest easternmost outpost of the late empire, a gorgeous tassel of the magic carpet. But for Vay, far though it was, and almost mythical to his metropolitan friends, the city must not be omitted from his study: so here he was, at last; too late, perhaps.

The young scholar, amongst his other accomplishments, took easily to languages: and once, when he was documenting Klagenfurt, he had pursued an awkward courtship with a young woman called Helena, who had been an earnest enthusiast of New Latin, and had decorated her notebooks and letters with its radiant sun. So he recognised the symbol and remembered what he knew of the language she had taught him. As he stood hesitating just inside the thick glass doors of the café, he realised how keen he was, suddenly, for the solace of sympathetic company after his tiresome journey, and so he advanced towards the two strangers. "*Ave*," he said, and asked if he might join them. Dr. Barusch hauled himself to his feet, welcomed him, beckoned for drinks, and asked eagerly if Vay had found his way here in answer to the New Latinist appeals he had issued.

The two had seen him when he first came in. They had observed a tired, uncertain young man whose flesh, in the dim light of the café, was of a strange and changeful olive-green. He was running his fingers through the blue-black hair that stuck out starkly against the drawn skin. Vay gently explained his mission.

"I have come to complete my study of the mascarons of the empire—of the late empire, that is to say the last four decades: but perhaps now late in another way too." He was not able to find the right word for "mascaron" in the re-invented language—it was not rich in recent terms of art—and so had used it as it was.

Dr. Barusch was uncertain of its meaning. At first he wondered if it might be some form of marshmallow that had hitherto escaped his attention, but this young man did not look a *bon vivant*. The doctor's fleshly face looked perplexed, and the dark eyebrows of Aurelian Zothe consulted together. Vay saw their puzzlement.

"Stone masks. They are found on many of our great public buildings. On cornices, or as keystones above doors or windows."

"Ah." The doctor made a little note in his pocket book.

"You may be out of luck, young man. I have never noticed any such features here. And I have to walk around a lot promoting our language, you see. I go slowly, as you can imagine . . . "—he indicated his girth—"so I have plenty of time to look around. But what sort of things would they be?"

The young man felt the weariness of his journey seeping even more insistently into his limbs. To come so far and to find nothing? Still, he knew that the untutored often did not see what was easily before their eyes. He had grey eyes like cinders, but glints of dying fire still sparked there at times.

"Well, for example, they might be a corn god or a harvest goddess on a bank; or Mercury, in his winged helmet, on the post office; or the spirits of Comedy and Tragedy on the theatre; lion's heads on the state buildings and so on. Here . . . "

He reached inside his dusty, scuffed brown suitcase and produced an album well-bound in a deep blue, then quickly flicked the pages. The figure playing his solitary game of circular chess looked up from his alcove, as if the riffling of the thick paper had altered his train of thought, his plotting of the black and white pieces.

"These were some very fine ones in Pressburg; these, quite unusual in Lemberg; and these, with a distinctive style, were in Trieste." From the pages, haughty brows, blind stone-socketed eyes, pointed ears and curling lips leapt out in his deft pencil renditions.

Zothe peered across at them, then stubbed out his black cigarette and shrugged. "I made the first or anyway the best street map of the city not long after I arrived. So I had to study the streets and buildings quite carefully. There is nothing of that kind here. But . . . " he held up his hand fleetingly to summon more drinks, "Stay awhile anyway. There is still much in the city to find."

The sun had hardened further by the time Michael Vay left his friends in the café and it seemed to draw out all the keen scents of the city, the rank odour of horse droppings, the heavy wafts of fried bread from wayside booths, the occasional bursts of over-ripe fruit from the piles laid on blankets by the country people, the musky smell of the many cats that prowled the streets, tails high; the deep loamy miasma coming up from the river; and infrequently a freshet from the far pines, or a waft of cinnamon or cloves from an arcade. All of these worked upon him to induce by turns revulsion or an unfathomable longing, so that by the time he reached the bare room of the hostel and unloaded at last his luggage, throwing his hat with relief upon the narrow bed, with its threadbare counterpane in the peasant style, he felt that he knew more of the city than any Baedeker could tell him.

Closing his paled eyelids, which were like flakes of fine china, he found sleep at last: and by the time he awoke, darkness had fallen. He sat up and wondered for a few moments where he was. Then, in a sudden inrush of recollections, he remembered his arrival and the conversation with the New Latinists in the café, and their assurance that he would find no mascarons here. With a surge of determination, he resolved to go out early in the morning and see for himself. He brushed down his clothes half-heartedly and reshaped his hat, so that they were ready for when he rose: then, with a quick piece of defiance, he searched out his sketchbook. He had never known any great city of the late empire not to possess at least some mascarons; he would find whatever was here, despite what they said. He flicked through the sketchbook once again and the limned masks seemed to leap from the page, the braid of a maiden's hair, the vine-leaves of a demi-god, the snarl of a lion and the snorting nostrils of a centaur, the strong neck and high cheekbones of an Olympian, the laurel wreath and lyre of a spirit of poetry, the calm cold stare of a goddess of wisdom. As the crisp white leaves flickered under his fingers, he caught sight of the only sketch in the book that was not of a stone mask, and he turned back to look at it. This was a drawing he had made of Helena, the Carinthian girl, her head and shoulders only, so that for a moment you might take it to be another picture of a deity or spirit. He gazed at it briefly. His pencil had captured the fine features of her cheekbones and brows, the rather stubborn set of her mouth, the fall of her white-gold hair around the nape of her neck, but it had not conveyed the gaze of her eyes at all, and Michael Vay searched his memory to bring their rather melancholy blue back into mind.

He remembered instead the day he had drawn the picture. They had quarrelled because her father would not let him see her very often: he was suspicious about his half-foreign ancestry. Vay had said she should simply leave and join him in his journeyings to the far cities of the empire: the idea had scandalised her. She had her own plan, her own work, anyway: her internationalist ideals. There might be service she could do at the League of Nations or at the headquarters of the Red Cross. In that birch grove in the bright green of the spring, by the white stream, she had allowed him a single chaste embrace. When he had heard of her again, it was from her sister. Helena was not in Switzerland, but at a sanatorium on the old imperial island of Zara, in the Adriatic, for its gentle warmth and ancient herbs. It were better, she said, that he did not write: she must not be unsettled. He had been far away in Galicia, at the most distant boundary of the empire, when the letter found him: none had ever followed, even though he had disobeyed the instruction not to write. Usually, from wherever he was, he had despatched a postcard: but whether they found her, he had never known. Once only, with precise efficiency, the postal service of the Empire had conspired to return a card to him at the field station from where he had addressed it. It was marked in regulation blue crayon with the terse message: "Not Known". He could not find out more: his military work had held him at first, and leave in those desperate harried days was out of the question. And after the war he felt the insistent call of his work, that he could not cease till he had seen and transfixed on the fine white pages the image of every mascaron the empire had.

The page fell from the light hold of his fingers. Sighing, he closed the book. The curfew in the hostel would now be in force for the night, yet he felt restless. He knew he must occupy his mind so that he did not become morbid, and thought what else he could do to prepare for his quest tomorrow. He took out his pocketbook to make notes, and saw a coloured sheet of paper he had placed with it.

Under the desk lamp he examined the map that Aurelian Zothe had given him. To the south were the cavalry barracks, botanical gardens, hospital; to the east the artillery fortress, the cemeteries of the various faiths; to the north an open heath and the railway station, with all its sidings; and to the west the grounds of the metropolitan's palace and the royal park. From these boundaries, a few utterly straight avenues led, with a fixity of purpose that suggested either a military or a ceremonial origin. But at its innermost heart, the city, he saw, was not in the least linear. As he tilted the map to the bloom of the light, he saw that the place was perhaps best understood by its squares, each linked by a reverie of lanes that even Zothe's skills sometimes struggled to capture. Most central of all was the Ring-Platz, where the wide radial roads led, and where the Café de l'Europe was situated; bigger but barer was the National-Platz (the nation now tactfully not specified); a slightly askew square, more a twisted diamond, was the Rudolf-Platz, and here, tinted green, was a Frans-Joseph-Platz. He smiled to himself: how many other cities had he visited, with just those same names? He would start from the Ring-Platz tomorrow and work outwards, much in the way, it came to him, the pieces reached out from that peculiar circular chess board.

As sleep at last overcame him that night, he saw the masks he had drawn hover before his eyes, fading one into another, until they all converged on one: Helena.

Before he left for the day, he glanced at the printed notices displayed upon a table in the entrance hall. He smiled to see that Dr. Barusch had succeeded in placing his New Latinist leaflet here, and looked idly at the announcements of concerts, plays, lectures, a Schiller evening, with readings also from the work of the new young poet Rilke, country dancing, church services, and a meeting of a group calling itself the New Force whose emblem was a barbed lance. Shrugging, he left all of these as they were, and went out into the apricot warmth of the morning.

Towards the end of the day he felt he had quartered as much of the central perimeter of the city as his feet could bear, and admitted to himself that his café acquaintances were right. There were no mascarons to be seen. Using Zothe's chart, he had found the major banking houses, the museum, the opera house, the state house, the post office, all imposing enough, and evidently built in the latter part of the last century when the region became a "crown land", with new privileges. Yet all were unadorned, and his drawing book had no additions. Vay felt the need again for friendly company and wondered about returning to the café in the Ring-Platz. Several times during the day, as he pursued his lonely searches, he had seemed to see, in a passer-by, a face, or more correctly a feature, he recognised: and a few times he had almost hailed them before the quick realisation blazed that he knew no-one here except the two he had met on the first day. This had happened so often that it began to trouble him as he thought about it now, so that he sat down on a bench under a chestnut tree and tried to gather his wits. His fingers fidgeted unbidden at the pages of his sketchbook. He glanced down idly at the page they had found. Then he looked with more concentration, frowning. That drawing, made he supposed in Pressburg some years ago, had the brow and the eye-shape of the poised woman he had seen

155

studying the programme outside the school of arts. With a quick flicker of the pages, he looked at more of his pictures. Nothing there, or there, or—yes, wait; the old man he had seen queuing outside the veterans' institute, here was his fierce snout and fine whiskers in a lion mask he had sketched once in Galicia. And there, further on in the album, was the dreamy gaze of a white stone Pierrot from a theatre in Linz, which he had seen in the eyes of a pale boy lolling by the fountains in the Rudolf-Platz.

Michael Vay closed the book slowly and shook his head. The heat of the city was oppressive and he had tired himself too much. Finding nothing of interest for his study, his eyes had betrayed him and placed the masks he wanted to see over the unexceptional faces of people in the streets. He must put a stop to that. What he needed was facts, not these fantasies. He thought he must consult some works of reference about the city, but by now the domed library had closed. He began to wander aimlessly in the byways close to the university: a swinging white sign with the symbol of an open book caught his attention.

Painted script in faded blue lettering told him that this was the establishment of Isidore Barleon, and that he was a Book Handler, as the official tongue quaintly put it. He pushed open the green-paned door and entered. Rows of volumes stretched out before him, like paper statues in some vast museum. In contrast to most such shops that Vay had entered before, this one was orderly. The books were neatly aligned on their shelves, there were none on the gnarled wooden floor, and instead of the fusty, mildewy smell normally encountered, there was a slight hint of cedarwood, perhaps from polish, or perhaps from the burning of resins.

Nor was the owner, as he had expected, a white-haired ancient. He was not so much older than himself, and he had a round, benevolent face with an inquisitive look that frail wire-framed glasses seemed to accentuate. He wore a blue smock. Vay asked him if there were any books on the city's history or architecture, and explained his particular interest.

"Yes, I see. No, I have nothing here on that theme. But may I look more closely at your book?" He pointed to the album of sketches Vay carried.

Michael Vay surrendered the volume to the young bookseller. The latter inspected the binding carefully and then turned over the pages. He took the book over to the door, which he opened wide to admit the glare of the day. Then he held up a page to the light, and then another.

"This is a very fine volume. You wouldn't sell it, I suppose?"

Vay shook his head. "My drawings." There were also other reasons.

Barleon signalled he understood. "Some must mean a great deal to you perhaps?"

When the young scholar did not reply, the bookseller held onto the book, as if reluctant to let it go.

"Where did you get it, if I may ask?"

Vay blinked. But there was something in the gentle warmth of the bookseller that made him willing to say a little more.

"My mother gave it to me when I first started my studies."

Barleon nodded. "I will tell you where she got it from, or where it first came from."

Vay had never given this very much thought. It was a sturdy, well-made book with good quality paper that took his pencillings well, that was all he knew.

"From Firenze. This binding, you see, is in the Moorish blue hide they cure so well there, knowing—and only they—the secret of its preparation. These endpapers—the plumed scarlet and gold design—that is typical of their work. But more particularly, this paper has the Florentine watermarks, you see?"

Still at the open door, he held up an unused page once more, and helped Vay see the impression of a flourish within the paper, a curving sigil of pale gold.

157

"Your mother chose well for you. You must tell her Isidore Barleon, the best, the most discerning bookseller in the city, said so."

The young scholar shuffled his feet in their cracked black shoes. "It won't be possible. She died in the influenza epidemic."

"I see." Barleon, he noted, did not offer any false sympathy. But he closed the book, pushed the door back in its place, and gently took him by the elbow to a chair by his desk at the end of the shop. There was a silence while the bookseller regarded him. Curiosity was evidently vying with sensitivity in his breast. The first at length took charge.

"Was she ever in Florence, do you know? They do not sell these books, you see, outside of it."

Vay sighed. "I am sure of it. She was half-Greek, she always told me, half-Triestine. She often went beyond the empire, to Salonika, say, to Ravenna once I know. She loved art—the masters, you know, not the modern things. I suppose she would not have omitted to go there. She would tweak me a little about these grotesques I drew. She wondered why I bothered with such baroque monstrosities, I suppose."

Barleon nodded. "Because you have done them all too well, my friend. These masks seem like real creatures, not just curves and lines of stone."

Vay started at this adroit observation, but he did not pretend to demur from the compliment to his art. He saw that here was one in whom he could confide his recent bizarre experiences. "Yes, I know. I even sometimes think I see them in the streets."

The bookseller exhaled slowly, then took off his flimsy spectacles and wiped them on a rag.

"In the streets? Here? In this city?"

The scholar nodded. "It is just a fancy. Perhaps I have stared at the sketches too long."

There was another pause. "Did you ever see them in any other city?"

Michael Vay quietly admitted he had not.

Aurelian Zothe collected an array of his maps in many languages from the printer and began his round of the black-and-gold tobacco kiosks to replenish the stocks and collect money from the sales. But at the first of these, run by a retired postmaster of the late empire, who still wore his service medals proudly, and addressed his customers with the correct honorific, he was met by a regretful shake of the head as he spread out his wares.

"They have ordered that we may only sell them now in the new official language," he said. "You will find all the other kiosks will be the same. I can take those but I cannot take the others. I am sorry: they all sold well enough, and the truth is that when people buy a map they often remember to buy other things too, so it was good for business. But now, no. They would dismiss me."

Zothe knew it would be futile to argue with a veteran official brought up on unquestioning obedience to authority, even in this far-flung city, and even though it was no longer the empire that made the rules (and it would never have made this rule either). There might be some vendors who would take a few of the unofficial maps on the sly: there might, indeed; for the city had a wonderful way with unconventional trade of all sorts, with markets that sprang up like mushrooms where you least expected. But his business would be severely reduced. Disconsolately, he asked for a packet of his black cigarettes and a box of Eidelweiss matches, and made a dejected round of his other traders, only to find that the old postmaster was quite right: they would only take those in the new official language.

The exile made his way to a favourite bench beneath a beech tree in the Rudolf-Platz and smoked thoughtfully.

The fountain made a soothing liquid patter. Jackdaws raised their rattling voices in the rooftops in their strange and secret language which seemed like the clatter of an aerial rosary. Cab horses plodded solemnly by, their drivers hunched as if asleep: and some undoubtedly were, for their nags knew every cobble of the city. Bearded priests in black soutanes, Talmud students with caps and corkscrew curls, clutching holy books, young men in the dapper costume of fencing fraternities, the strong-featured mountain women with their embroidered waistcoats, silent heavy cart-drivers bringing wood-loads to the city, and brown-eyed ragged boys, running between the sunlight and the shade, all passed before his contemplating gaze. He thought that he had never seen such a medley of humanity before, not even in his days in the cities on the shores of the Caspian Sea, or in Constantinople when the waves of refugees flooded the old Byzantine capital. But if now there was to be one language only allowed, and that not the simple neutral European tongue that old Barusch loved, he could see that the city would change. He sighed. It was time, he reflected, to think about his next move.

The architectural scholar had not given up his quest for any quaint carvings in the city, and his wanderings soon took him to remoter and obscurer quarters. For several days he gazed upon even the more minor public buildings, but the craft of the mascaron was nowhere to be seen. On the other hand, just as on the first day of his search, he seemed to keep glimpsing passers-by whose features struck him as strangely familiar: and each time the recollection of the shape of their eyes, or the curve of their lips, or the twist of their ears, would take him to a sketch he had once made in another city. One evening, his increasingly desultory footsteps took him to the east of the city, far out beyond the frequented highways, and as dusk descended like the powder of a fine rare blue spice, he heard a murmurous undercurrent of mingled noises, and began to make out ahead sudden surges of fire.

He came upon an open cobbled space, a square he had not seen before, surrounded by crooked, lichened houses which leaned against each other like drunken old men seeking mutual support. They had roofs like shabby hats and dull plaster walls like patched overcoats. Their narrow windows were gloomed over as if an alcoholic haze had indeed descended upon them, and they seemed to present a sympathy in stone for the fuddled old men stumbling about in the square. The scene was lit by braziers heaped with red embers and cressets whose iron spars rose upward and curled out like the golden flames they contained. They cast just enough light to see the dark shapes of things, but not the detail, except when a figure passed close by them, when all the hollows and prominences of the face would be fleetingly illumined. The place was thronged with carts, stalls, booths, makeshift tents, and Vay could smell an overwhelming array of produce, from the tart, sickly stench of newly released blood from the butcher's booth to the cloying, honeyish aroma of the sweet-cake quoits that boys carried on long pointed sticks like wands, tempting passers-by. Vay took one and ate it hungrily, passing a coin to the street arab, who nodded thanks. The scholar watched him as he walked away to ply his trade further among the milling grey figures. There was something in the curl of the ears above the grimy collar which nudged a memory in him, and he knew he would find this child too in his book.

This, then, Vay understood was the half-fabled Night Market, which appeared in the city as if spontaneously, and here, as well as the things of the day, one could buy whatever was better acquired or enjoyed during darkness. At intervals, whichever authorities happened to be in charge of the city would make half-hearted attempts to identify those who ran the market and close it down: but so far it had always sprung up again, like a rank fungus in the darkness, in some other secret quarter.

As Vay wandered cautiously around the square he began to see that this market of the dark resolved itself into different zones of influence. Here might be found fate, fortune and faith, the chances that men take with their soul. Travelling gamers spread out three aces, two black, one red, for the visiting goatherds to guess at, deftly flicking the red ace between their fingers. Players were allowed to win sufficiently often to tempt others: but the silver in the shuffler's satchel easily grew the most. Prophecies were to be had by the palm, the cards, the glass, the skull, or in little written snatches of paper. Stalls laid out with lace and ribbons sold pewter-framed souvenirs of the melancholy young emperor and old bald walrus-whiskered Frans-Josef, or crudely painted ikons of the dead tsar and his family. There were holy things said to have stranger provenance still: a musty Tibetan prayer-book; an Armenian medallion; a pendant with a hair of Queen Tamar of the Georgians; a fingernail of the Veiled Prophet; a tincture said to be strengthened by the seed of Tamurlane. Even the most sacred has its price and the stallholders were ready for hard haggling before parting with their treasures. They seldom made the mistake of selling the same rare item twice in a night, but on other nights it might be found to have miraculously multiplied.

In a corner of the square, creatures were kept trussed, caged or leashed and their roars or cries added a sharp scimitar of slicing sound to the high cacophony of the market, at intervals riding above the bawling of the night sellers, the slurred singing of the drunks and the keening violin of a street musician. Within stinking alleys and doorways and in dank and unlit courtyards the oldest trade of all was carried on, and it too was accompanied by squeals and grunts, vying with the shouts of the captive beasts.

In another zone, contraband barrels and angular glass vessels held spirits it was hard to get in the cafés, and there were chests of tobacco that the black and gold kiosks of the state monopoly never sold, and opiates and resins that offered oblivion or wild visions, for a price, and for a time. Vay found himself repulsed by much that he saw, but unable to break free of its fascination. A drunkard lurched against him, nearly toppling him over, and murmured a heartfelt, fume-ridden contrition. He insisted that the young scholar should share a draught from the corroded lips of his spirit flask. Vay took a gulp to be rid of him. The hot raw spirit burnt his throat and rushed to his nostrils and it was all he could do not to gag. The drunk clapped him on the back and thrust him forcibly into the path of an itinerant preacher exhorting the revellers to desist from sin and prepare for the coming apocalypse. He took hold of Vay by the lapels and asked him if he had seen the red clouds ride. It seemed to be a question of the utmost urgency and import and the man stared vehemently into his eyes as if he could read the answer there.

Vay freed himself as gently as he could, but the fumes from the drunkard's flask were now rising to his mind and he knew a desperate need to have more. He pushed his way to one of the contraband stands and seized a vial at random, throwing a handful of coins at the narrow-faced owner. For a brief moment an innate caution returned and, removing the stopper, he sniffed the pale, pink, bitter liquid within. A scent as of blighted roses came to him overpoweringly, as if he were in a swoon in a ruined Persian garden, and he wanted to be possessed by this deep, rare ichor, to have it thrill through his veins. He craned back his pale viridian throat and took the elixir upon his tongue, then swallowed greedily. It was as if a plucked scarlet rose had shivered down his throat, like the sleek blades of the sword-swallowers: yet its cruel thorns of green-bronze had caught and clung to his inner flesh as it descended into him. The heady pleasure and the sharp pain mingled into one and he called for another vial, relishing again the perfumed breath and the burning rasp, as the rose spirit took hold of him from within.

He glared about him with gleaming eyes at the heaving throng, the men and women of the night. He saw ex-soldiers still in the torn uniforms of different armies, sullenly begging, or performing pathetic tricks with whatever limbs or senses were left to them; he saw barely clothed gutter children jostling to pick up whatever glitter fell onto the slimy cobbles or streaked street paths; he saw bedraggled, brown-limbed beckoning women laugh at him from the shadows; there were lepers exposing their weeping sores to provoke pity; and the grey-bearded sellers of the grave dust of the saints and prophets were solemnly hawking their sacred wares in blue paper packets, inscribed with strange stark letters. And then he thought he saw, among them all, another face he knew from his book; the only face not made of stone; he saw her wavering on the edge of the crowd, like a white candle; it was the slightest glimpse, yet even within the fevered embrace of the distilled rose he knew it to be her. Reason and hope surged back to him and he told himself she surely must have come to the city in answer to Dr. Barusch's campaign, and (like himself) got lost and drawn in to the vile commotion of the Night Market.

The high rising wail of the street violin, the yelping of the caged animals, the urgings of the vendors and the coarse cries of the crowds crashed like dark waves lashed by a fierce storm upon the stone square, and Vay forced himself with a fervent urgency to seek a way through, pushing aside all the surging bodies. He found himself thrust against their angered faces, which lunged before him. Here was the wide lascivious leer of a satyr, here the sly smile of a faun, the bellied cheeks and bulging eyes of a silenus, or a face with the terrible allure of a lamia, or an old man with the blind and dreadful stare of a dead god. But no longer were they mute: harsh laughter, a sinister hissing, a hollow gong-like groaning, an obscene whispering issued from their lips. And a stench like the deepest corruption came upon him, banishing the scented ichors of the rose spirit and filling all his senses and even his flesh with its wormy miasma.

Still deep within his mind, his reason revolted, and he shook his head. Suppressing the panic that still lunged at him from all sides, he told himself these could not be the faces of those who came to the Night Market, no matter how brutal some of them might be. He was being made to see some other scene, a mad lupanar of all the darkest mythic instincts lurking in the underworlds of the empire. But surely there were other urges too that he could call upon? He called to mind the grave wisdom carved into the eyes and brows of the face of Athena in the great museum in the capital: she too was preserved in his book. He remembered the Apollo on the admiralty building facing the Adriatic at Trieste, with his far-seeing eyes and the golden hair the sculptor had captured so finely. He threw out the thought of their masks raised before him like shields, and imagined them lowering their gaze upon the writhing throng, who seemed to cower under their stare. Then there came over him a simple certainty of his way through, and he fumbled in his book for the drawing he had made from the face inscribed into the keystone above the door of the citadel for the Imperial Equerries in Prague. He found the mask of the youth with wings on his helmet and an enigmatic smile on his stone lips, and he said aloud, though he did not know how the words came to him: Great Hermes, Guide of Souls; and once more, much louder; and again, like a call echoing in a mountain valley. All the gross noise of the market was silenced for the fragments of a moment and the crowd around him, whether they were human or semi-human to his gaze, shrank away from him, as one who is possessed.

Clinging hard still to his book of mascarons, he threw himself through the opening, until he staggered out at last into the margins of the market, where she had been. He had tried to keep that pale form before him, but the faces of the others, those gross clawing forms, had obscured his sight, and now she was nowhere to be seen. He ran around the perimeter of the market repeatedly, he plunged into the backstreets and courtyards, he tried calling her name, over and over. But it was to no avail. At last, as the red scars of dawn revealed themselves, he found himself too exhausted to search further and slept propped on a bench under a wanly flickering lamp.

The noon sun saw Michael Vay pushing open the door of Isidore Barleon's bookshop again. Then he stepped back, aghast. The calm order that had so impressed him when he had visited before had been torn apart. The bookcases leaned awry at crazy angles. Mounds of books had been doused with water or oil: some had black curling leaves where flames had started but not taken. The bookseller greeted him with a grim nod as he moved quietly to put things right, patiently and deliberately taking up each book, and tending to its wounds. Vay did what he could to help.

"I had visitors," Barleon said. "They loved books so much they threw them in the air in delight. Then they wanted to light a fire to proclaim their ardour. But books are harder to burn than you think. Come, that is enough for the moment. I'm glad to see you. Have you found any masks yet? Or have they found you?"

His visitor recounted what he had seen at the Night Market. Barleon adjusted his spectacles and nodded. He did not try to persuade his visitor that the scenes had all been a delusion, but calmly accepted what Vay haltingly described.

"I wanted to know," said Michael Vay quietly, "what more you can tell me about this book my mother gave me."

The bookseller sighed. "Very little. It will have been made, I think, from the watermark, by a master of the guild of stationers in Firenze, a confraternity who had many trades besides paper. It's said they date from the time of Cosimo Vecchi: but certainly some of their skills are still respected, and secret today. Possibly they had some of those crafts from the Saracen, or from the Sephardi, or the Byzantines: Cosimo at least was unprejudiced when it came to the pursuit of wisdom."

Barleon became thoughtful. In the shop, there was the shuffling sound of books settling down in their places, as if drawing succour from each other. A few stray pages from a book as yet unrestored riffled where it lay open.

"Yes, they knew how to make books of power, that is true," he resumed. "But why do you suppose what you have seen is the book's doing? It is you who conjured all those stone spirits onto the page so well, from all the corners of the late empire. Perhaps you have simply released them into the city."

Vay's olive-green face grew troubled as he struggled with his friend's strange idea.

"And Helena?" he asked at last. "Is she also only a spirit?"

Barleon touched his shoulder, but would not reply.

As the young scholar left he saw a crude scratch-mark upon the wall: a barbed lance.

In the succeeding days, Michael Vay searched for the Carinthian girl throughout the city, tramping every broad thoroughfare, every narrow twisting street, the secluded squares with their bright-barked cherry trees, the staunch serries of mustard-yellow merchants' houses, the heaped-up slums, the remote lanes where a few stray houses lingered as if uncertain whether to belong to the city or not, with their allotment of vegetable garden, whiskered goat, old wells or pumps, racks of drying herbs. He no longer looked for the stone masks now, on the buildings or in the flesh of the city folk, but still in the sudden turn of a face he felt he saw hints of the features of those in his book. But even with his obsession in the urgent quest for the pale young woman that he had glimpsed at the verge of the Night Market, he could not help noticing other changes to the city. Certain shops and offices had a gaping black star where windows had been smashed in, or ugly daubs of red paint, or the stark sign of the barbed lance. Books, journals and sheet music could be found heaped and torn in the street, and once he saw a seven-branched candelabra twisted and dented and thrust upside down in a soil bank. When he went out to the eastern quarter where the cemeteries were, searching for her, or her spirit, even there, he saw that some gravestones had been broken or uprooted, and the pebbles that had been left as offerings had been strewn among weeds. Increasingly in the streets he witnessed the parading of men with the hard faces, the stiff throats and tautened cheek-muscles, the grim mouths, the Medusan stare, of the masks he had sometimes seen of Mars.

It was some time before he ventured into the Café de l'Europe once again, taking Isidore Barleon with him. The ornate doors and the inviting aromas, the settled order of the customers in their regular places, the cloaked figure bent in concentration over his circular chess board, studying the pieces in their segments, were unchanged. But there seemed fewer people, and the quiet murmur that had pervaded the place before was now more restive, with sometimes raised voices and the slap of hands upon the table tops in irrepressible emphasis of the words spoken. They sat silently together, appreciating the rare aura of the café. The bookseller asked for a glass of persimmon juice. Cautiously, Vay ordered only a mineral water, the Swabian spa water called Castalia, in its blue Cubist bottle. The waiter poured the little white cascade into a green-tinged glass and for a brief flicker of time Vay remembered the white brook and the green grove where he and Helena had last met, as if the moment had been recreated in miniature. The murmur of the café died away and he saw her clearly, her white form, her beautiful troubled face, the frown that he had loved. But it was for an instant only and the tinkling of a tea spoon broke in upon his brief reverie. And it came upon him with a bitter certainty that this was now the only Helena he would ever see or know, the girl remembered in such fleeting visions, through all the intervals of the years.

He looked up to see Dr. Julius Barusch lowering his ample form into place at his usual table, and gesturing them to come over and join him. The doctor took out his little radiant sun desk flag and placed it with a punch upon the marble top. In answer to Vay's weary questions, he said that no, he had not recruited a young woman named Helena to his New Latinist plans for the city, neither from Klagenfurt nor from Zara, and not from Geneva either. The truth was that his campaign was faltering. He himself had been banned from lecturing in the pan-European language at the university, or from distributing his leaflets, and the flag could not be flown from any public building. The desk flag was an act of small defiance, but he didn't doubt that soon they would tell him to stop that too. The New Force was abroad in the city and it did not condone his internationalist ideas. He shook his great head and although the wobbling of his jowls had a comical aspect to it, still Vay saw the sorrow in his eyes.

Soon Aurelian Zothe sauntered through the doors and took his place, lighting another black cigarette. He had a sardonic grin upon his angular face, and his vivid necktie was clasped by a bright yellow opal. He had created a new satirical map of the city, which he spread out before them. In

169

its centre there was a round palisade of lances and within that an empty void, a white space. Above the streets, great ornate arrows burst out from the city in all directions and next to each was printed a destination: Zürich, London, Paris, New York, Jerusalem, Salonika, Alexandria. The arrows were all decorated: they took with them in their soaring flight, stylised books, music clefs, theatrical masks, laboratory retorts, a caduceus, jackdaws, chess pieces, playing cards, a tottering pile of sweet quoits: and, dark wings outstretched, the double eagle of the old empire.

"They will hound you down for that, Aurelian," said Dr. Barusch tenderly. Zothe shook his head and jabbed a forefinger, still clinging to one side of a cigarette, at a little figure on the map. They bent to look. Even in miniature, there was no mistaking the triangular face and the dark taper dangling from its mouth. Zothe was on the arrow bound for Alexandria.

The mapmaker looked at his friends questioningly. "Care to join me? They say the cafés are good there, and the government so inefficient that it can hardly ever make up its mind who to persecute, and even then it doesn't do it properly."

Beneath the seeming insouciance, his companions at the table knew that the thin-faced mapmaker would be sorry to leave the city he had learned to know so well, whose narrowest streets and loneliest squares he had discovered and charted. There was a dimming in his pale blue eyes, the tiredness of the constant exile. He tried to cover this up from his friends by making a to-do of relighting his spluttering black cigarette, and exhaling the silver-blue fumes heavily. "The tobacco will be better there too," he added.

Dr. Barusch, after a pause, clapped his friend on the shoulder. "I am sorry, Aurelian, sorry indeed. But I am not sure the Alexandrian climate would do my health much good. And I doubt that they are ready for New Latin, for all their ancient classical past. No, it is back to the centre of Europe for me." He borrowed a pen from his friend and drew a radiant sun on an airship (himself) bound for Zürich. There was a gentle laughter at this little caricature, but a laughter that did not alter the quiet sorrow that had descended upon them. "But," added Barusch, a little mischievously, for he knew and tolerated his friend's half-heartedness about his cherished language, "we shall be able to practice our New Latin when we write to each other, no? The sights there will surely stretch your vocabulary, eh?"

The bookseller in his turn shook his head. He knew the risks, he said, and he did not blame his friends for leaving while they could. There might come a day, he knew, when he would not even have that choice. But, his frail glasses gleaming, he drew his bookshop on the map, where it was now and where it had been for many years. Where it would stay. Indeed, he said, he would welcome assistance. There was, it seemed, a great deal to do in book restoration these days. So many volumes had the habit of being torn from their spines, of leaping into pyres, of ending in refuse heaps, of being smeared with terse, coarse messages. It was like having wayward children: and after such escapades they needed especial care.

Michael Vay let the pages of his Florentine drawing book flutter through his fingers. Their breath rippled the new map so that it seemed like an Arabian carpet about to take flight, as if the spirits of all the masks he had drawn, from all the far-flung cities of the late Empire, were suspiring together to help it float upon its way.

And now he knew that his work was over.

Acknowledgements

My thanks to R. B. Russell for the photograph
that inspired Jason Zerrillo's cover art;
and to the following editors and publishers for
the first appearances of these stories:

"Carden in Capaea"
was first published in *Strange Tales II*,
edited by Rosalie Parker. Tartarus Press, 2007.

"The Autumn Keeper"
was first published in *Cinnabar's Gnosis*,
edited by D.T. Ghetu. Ex Occidente Press, 2009.

"The Bookshop in Nový Svět" and
"The Dawn at Tzern" were first published in
The Nightfarers. Ex Occidente Press, 2009.

"A Walled Garden on the Bosphorus" and
"The Mascarons of the Late Empire" were first published
in *The Mascarons of the Late Empire & Other Studies*.
Ex Occidente Press, 2010.

"The Unrest at Aachen"
was first published in *Delicate Toxins*,
edited by John Hirschhorn-Smith.
Side Real Press, 2011.

"The Amber Cigarette", "The Ka of Astarakahn", and
"A Certain Power" were first published in
The Peacock Escritoire. Ex Occidente Press, 2011.

"The Original Light"
was first published in *This Hermetic Legislature*,
edited by D.P. Watt & D.T. Ghetu.
Ex Occidente Press, 2012.

About the Author

Mark Valentine's stories have been selected for *Best British Short Stories* edited by Nicholas Royle, *Best New Horror* edited by Stephen Jones, *The Mammoth Books of Ghost Stories* edited by Richard Dalby, and the *Ghosts & Scholars* books edited by Rosemary Pardoe, as well as for many other anthologies. Along with Swan River Press, he also publishes with other independent imprints such as Tartarus Press (UK), Sarob Press (France), and Zagava (Germany). His books include studies of Arthur Machen and the diplomat and fantasist Sarban, and essays on book-collecting and the esoteric. He also edits *Wormwood*, a journal of the fantastic.

SWAN RIVER PRESS

Founded in 2003, Swan River Press is an independent publishing company, based in Dublin, Ireland, dedicated to gothic, supernatural, and fantastic literature. We specialise in limited edition hardbacks, publishing fiction from around the world with an emphasis on Ireland's contributions to the genre.

www.swanriverpress.ie

"Handsome, beautifully made volumes . . .
altogether irresistible."

– Michael Dirda, *Washington Post*

"It [is] often down to small, independent, specialist presses
to keep the candle of horror fiction flickering . . ."

– Darryl Jones, *Irish Times*

"Swan River Press has emerged as one of the most inspiring
new presses over the past decade. Not only are the books
beautifully presented and professionally produced, but they
aspire consistently to high literary quality and originality,
ranging from current writers of supernatural/weird fiction
to rare or forgotten works by departed authors."

– Peter Bell, *Ghosts & Scholars*

SEVENTEEN STORIES

Mark Valentine

Mark Valentine's stories have been described by critic Rick Kleffel as "consistently amazing and inexplicably beautiful". He has been called "A superb writer, among the leading practitioners of classic supernatural fiction" by Michael Dirda of the *Washington Post*, and his work is regularly chosen for year's best and other anthologies.

This selection offers previously uncollected or hard to find tales in the finest traditions of the strange and fantastic. As well as tributes to the masters of the field, Valentine provides his own original and otherworldly visions, with what *Supernatural Tales* has called "the author's trademark erudition" in "unusual byways of history, folklore and general scholarship". Opening a book will never seem quite the same again after encountering this curious volume of *Seventeen Stories . . .*

*"Valentine is a writer in love with
the great tradition of the weird tale."*

– Supernatural Tales

*"[Valentine's] is attentive to place and to
the power of obsession, but one of his true gifts is
an ability to suggest modes of artistic expression."*

– The Endless Bookshelf

THE SATYR
& Other Tales

Stephen J. Clark

In the final throes of the Blitz, Austin Osman Spare is the only salvation for Marlene, an artist escaping a traumatic past. Wandering Southwark's ruins she encounters Paddy Hughes, a fugitive of another kind. Falling under Marlene's spell Hughes agrees to seek out her lost mentor, the man she calls The Satyr. Yet Marlene's past will not rest as the mysterious Doctor Charnock pursues them, trying to capture the patient she'd once caged. *The Satyr* is a tale inspired by the life and ethos of sorcerer and artist Austin Osman Spare.

Another three novellas of occult enchantment follow: a bookseller discovers that his late wife knew the Devil, in the Carpathian Mountains refugees shelter in a museum devoted to a forgotten author, and in Prague a portraitist must paint a countess whose appearance is never the same twice.

*"This book will adorn your shelves, where it will be
at ease in shadowy converse with your copies of À Rebours,
The Picture of Dorian Gray, The Great God Pan."*

– Mark Valentine

*"Clark's subtle prose, vivid and disturbing imagery,
and the concepts he weaves into his stories make
them irresistible to those whose senses
have been jaded by more common fare."*

– *Black Static*

WRITTEN BY DAYLIGHT

John Howard

Sunsets in a London suburb, and a transformation into an Earthly paradise; paths winding through a Transylvanian palace gardens, and an obsessed journey towards a Mediterranean dream; a city so ancient that even its total disappearance has been forgotten, and an island of shifting sands that can never be truly mapped . . . The vivid and diverse settings of these stories are façades obscuring reality for the exiles and outcasts who find their way into them. Seemingly born out of time and place, they seek the right routes to bring them to where they want to be, but there are many diversions on the way. In these stories of haunted landscapes and intimidating cities many possibilities confront the unwary, but there is usually only one choice to be made.

"Howard's work is both delicate and powerful."

– The Agony Column

"If there is a unifying theme here it is the transience of existence, from the individual to the social and even the geographical . . . not only well-written but also offer remarkable ideas."

– Supernatural Tales

"Most of these tales are so subtle as to defy any category of the strange at all, but reward re-reading and are all the greater for it."

– The Pan Review